The Facts Behind
The Most Controversial War
Of Our Time

MYTH:
The U.S. War effort was spearheaded by elite
helicopter-borne troops.

REALITY:
The bulk of the war was fought by straight-leg
infantrymen, unromantically slogging it out in
the bush.

MYTH:
North Vietnam's General Giap was the great
military genius of the war.

REALITY:
Giap's inflexible overreliance on massed human
wave assaults nearly proved fatal at Khe Sanh and
in the 1968 Tet Offensive.

MYTH:
Tet as a major Communist victory.

REALITY:
The Communist attacks were actually suicidal,
costing as many as 50,000 dead and failing to
ignite the predicted popular uprisings.

MYTH:
The Vietnam War, however painful,
is history.

The war continues   n
a death struggle   s
Cambodi

BATTLEFRONT VIETNAM

TOM CARHART

Original title:

BATTLES AND CAMPAIGNS IN VIETNAM

WARNER BOOKS

A Time Warner Company

WARNER BOOKS EDITION

Copyright © 1984 by Bison Book Corporation

This Warner Books Edition is published by arrangement with
Brompton Books Corporation, 15 Sherwood Place, Greenwich,
CT 06830

Cover design: Don Puckey
Cover photos: U.S. Army

Warner Books, Inc.
666 Fifth Avenue
New York, N.Y. 10103

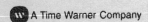 A Time Warner Company

Printed in the United States of America

First Warner Books Printing: February, 1991

10 9 8 7 6 5 4 3 2 1

CONTENTS

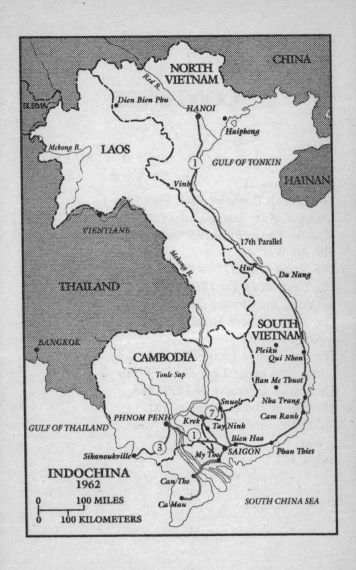

INTRODUCTION

On 1 May, 1975, the Republic of Vietnam, better known to most Americans simply as South Vietnam, fell to North Vietnam, and simply disappeared politically into what became a reunited nation of Vietnam run by ardent Communists. Many years later, a certain amount of confusion persists among American citizens that can be summed up in the question: what really happened over there? During the war, the White House and virtually all U.S. military leaders kept telling us that they/we were winning. But then somehow, after our troops were withdrawn—in response to the jagged domestic political unrest and dissatisfaction that broke this country open like an overripe watermelon—the forces of South Vietnam were defeated and the Communists took over. If we really had been winning militarily, how could that have happened?

Karl von Clausewitz was a highly regarded Prussian general who fought against Napoleon. But he is best remembered as a military theoretician and philosopher whose writings have offered leaders of later ages insights into apparently insoluble problems they have faced. It seems to me that one of his comments sheds light on our situation:

It is clear that war is not a mere act of policy, but a true political instrument, a continuation of political activity by other means. The political object of the war is the goal, war is the means of reaching it, and means can never be considered in isolation from their purpose. No one starts a war—or rather, no one in his right mind ought to do so—without first being clear in his mind what he intends to achieve by that war and how he intends to conduct it.

The political realities that underlie war in its onset, conduct, and outcome are often much more complex than are initially apparent to the casual observer. For instance, the political objective or goal of the war in Vietnam was never terribly clear not only to disinterested observers, but even to many of the crucially involved participants. The larger fact that American forces were supposed to be serving as some sort of insulation force that would protect the civilian population of South Vietnam from the external Communist threat was never realistically considered by many American soldiers who were supposed to be doing the actual fighting.

To understand that, it is important to realize that the average age of an American infantryman fighting in the Vietnam war was nineteen, as compared to twenty-six in World War II. While I was a commissioned officer myself, an "old man" of twenty-three, I was also rather naive in the ways of the world, and the age and so experience of sergeants bespake wisdom, enlightenment, an attainable path to survival. The official motto of my unit, the 101st Airborne Division, in Vietnam was "stay alert, stay alive," and the guidelines we accepted from "old-timers" when we arrived in-country were more guttural but ran along the same lines.

We repeated these slogans, mantralike, whether we had any first-hand experience to support them or not, for they established a sense of "us-against-them." To my knowledge, no formal effort was ever made to genuinely educate the average soldier on the subtle distinctions between our allies and our enemies.

When the official political line on the meaning and value of our role in Vietnam was silence, then the safest place to go for guidelines was to the wise and worldly sergeants, one of whose primary roles in war was keeping their men alive. While such psychological guidelines to the troops may have kept many of them alert and so accomplished this goal, the fact that such word was allowed to be spread is some indication of the attitudes of our military and civilian commanders.

Thus, the men who literally laid their lives on the line in this war only rarely had access to even the ill-defined and cloudy reasons it was being fought as it was, reasons about which our political and military leaders were never in full agreement themselves. In the immediate wake of South Vietnam's fall, public interest in such political realities—or indeed, in the flawed military efforts that had been made to carry out political directions and attain political goals—was slight at best.

The common reaction to the fall of South Vietnam within the American government, even in the supposedly apolitical ranks of the professional military, was generally to whistle bravely on through the dark and attempt to turn the historical page as quickly and smoothly as possible. The triumph then crowed from the rooftops by some Americans who had opposed, often at considerable personal cost, the U.S. military presence in Vietnam, however, made this charade somewhat more difficult to carry off in anything even approaching a convincing manner.

When it became clear a decade or so later that the predictions of misery for the peoples of Indochina condemned to lives of slavery under the tenets of Marxist/Leninist/Maoist theory were coming true, that literally millions of Southeast Asians were abandoning all and jumping into the sea, genuinely risking their lives in an often vain effort to escape the tyranny that had fallen over Indochina, even those Americans who had opposed U.S. troops in Vietnam fell strangely quiet. Americans of all political stripes were left dazed and silenced, still reeling from unexpected and poorly understood political body blows.

By 1990, however, a decade and a half after the fall, enough time seems to have passed for us to take a somewhat dispassionate look at some of the realities of the Vietnam war.

One such reality emerges immediately, and that is the meaning of the often heard political comment that "Vietnam is the first war the United States has ever lost." While that is a true statement, its meaning is generally misunderstood. For while it is true that we "lost" the Vietnam war in the sense that we failed to attain the political goals which caused us to involve our military there, we did not lose the *military* war that was waged in Vietnam. Throughout the roughly seven-year period from 1965 until 1972 when U.S. units were deployed in Vietnam, there is not a single incident when any American unit larger than company-sized (roughly one hundred men) was "defeated" and captured or killed by the military forces of our Communist adversary. Thus, the statement that we "lost" the Vietnam war, particularly when the Vietnam war is viewed as a traditional military war, can be misleading.

In military circles, one comment on the Vietnam war that has gained currency is: "We won the war, but lost the peace." Though the reasonable man might expect at least some rationalization from that quarter, the line is not far off the mark. When U.S. forces were actively involved in fighting the war—until late 1972—Communist attacks were generally stymied, and their forces were roundly defeated and eventually driven from virtually all populated areas of South Vietnam. After Americans had been withdrawn, however, the Communists once again began their buildup, only this time with impunity, and they eventually overwhelmed the numerically smaller South Vietnamese forces whose flow of logistics and supplies from the U.S. had been slowed to a trickle and then stopped altogether.

This larger military perspective has been generally slighted in most historical treatments of the Vietnam war. Yet, while it is difficult and misleading to separate military experiences from their political roots and causes, this is sometimes the only way to get a candid and accurate picture of what actually happened on the ground in a war zone.

That is particularly the case with respect to the Vietnam war, whose military aspects were generally concealed from the American public by an enormous cloud of political distortion and exaggeration intentionally created by strongly biased political players on both sides. The unfortunate historical fallout from this internecine political war is that the actual events in Vietnam have been largely obscured as a function of it, and few Americans have any real feel for the way the war was actually fought on the ground and in the air above Indochina.

It is time to change that historical misperception. This book deals exclusively with the war as it was actually fought in Vietnam, trying as much as possible to ignore the political thunderstorm that often underlay it both in the United States and elsewhere in the world. We begin with the French experience at the Battle of Dien Bien Phu in 1954 and proceed to the early advisory effort, and the first major fight between high-tech, helicopter-borne troops of the American 1st Cavalry (Airmobile) and hardened veterans of North Vietnamese regular forces. American forces won these early rounds, and it became apparent to the Communists that they could not stand toe-to-toe with strongly supported U.S. forces and slug it out, so they changed their approach. Chapter Three deals with this reality, when powerful and ponderous American forces were deployed to surround and sweep a known enemy base area, but came up with nothing and couldn't seem to understand why the out-gunned Communists didn't want to fight.

The fourth and fifth chapters take closeup looks at the different air and naval wars that occurred side by side and often in support of the ground war. Chapter Six covers the 1968 Communist Tet Offensive that exploded across the land, and Chapters Seven and Eight cover separately the major battles for Hue and Khe Sanh—the latter to be compared with Dien Bien Phu.

Chapter Nine covers the Cambodian incursion of 1970 that disturbed so many Americans, particularly on college campuses, but describes many aspects of the operation that were simply unknown back in "The World," as we fondly referred to the United States. Chapter Ten covers the South Vietnamese effort to invade Laos and cut the Ho Chi Minh Trail and how a lack of leadership and training more than anything else turned what started as a bold strike into a badly bungled debacle.

Chapter Eleven deals with the major conventional invasion of South Vietnam by most of the North Vietnamese army, on three different points of attack and using some five hundred tanks. While no American fighting troops were involved in stopping and repelling this invasion, massive U.S. airpower seems to have turned the tide. Chapter Twelve covers how in 1975 the thinly stretched South Vietnamese defenses simply crumbled before the slightest nudge by North Vietnamese forces and South Vietnam disappeared to be joined to North Vietnam as a unified nation ruled from Hanoi.

Finally, Chapter Thirteen covers the period after 1975, when the war seemed to smolder on, with the Vietnamese caught in a death struggle with other Asian states, first Cambodia and then the People's Republic of China.

This overview of the Vietnam war as it was actually fought is intended to give readers an understanding of the war as a military conquest and of Vietnam as one of the world's primary battlefronts.

THE FRENCH
DEBACLE

Dien Bien Phu

The first great battle of the Vietnam War in modern times—Dien Bien Phu—was fought in 1954, and the Western Power involved was France, not the United States. Understanding this battle and how it relates to the others that will follow requires some brief historical overview of Indochina in modern times.

During the 19th century, the French military began to assert itself in Indochina, primarily in support of French merchants and missionaries. In 1847 French naval forces bombarded the port of Danang and landed troops to suppress the anti-Catholic policies of a local ruler. All of Cochinchina—the fertile Mekong Delta and flatlands around Saigon—was soon brought under French control, and Cambodia became a French protectorate. Between 1883 and 1893, the French 'Indochinese Union' was completed, as Laos also became a protectorate and French forces conquered Annam (central Vietnam, whose ancient capital was Hue) and Tong King or Tonkin (northern Vietnam with Hanoi as capital).

The area was alive with ethnic rivalries: the Indian cultural pressures of the south conflicted with the Chinese tendencies of the north, and further tension from the Khmers and the small mountain tribes called 'Montagnards' by the French kept the brew simmering. French colonialists shrewdly played one ethnic group against the other, using swift military action as required to administer a bountiful string of colonies through the 1930s. Whatever nationalist opposition existed was quickly and easily suppressed as it appeared, mainly because such causes addressed narrow ethnic concerns. Nguyen Ai Quoc, an Annamese firebrand, founded the Indochinese Communist Party while in exile in Hong Kong in 1930, but his support at home was very limited. He took the name Ho Chi Minh and traveled to China, where he was trained by Mao Tse-tung and awaited the moment to return home and launch a Communist revolution.

In 1940 France fell to a German invasion within 30 days, and the German-controlled Vichy Government took over administration of the nation and its colonies. Almost immediately, Japan—an ally of Germany—took advantage of France's puppet status and gained the right to deploy its troops in Indochina, and used its airports and harbors in its fight against the Chinese. Nominally, the French retained administrative control of Indochina, but their authority was clearly limited.

This was what Ho Chi Minh had long awaited, and he soon founded the League for the Independence of Vietnam, or Viet Minh, and launched active military resistance against the French and Japanese from the mountains of Tonkin. He was joined by his Communist colleague, Vo Nguyen Giap, who became the field commander of his armed forces. They adopted Mao Tse-tung's three-stage plan for revolutionary war, the first stage of which requires political recruitment of the peasant masses, establishing solid bases with them and training recruits militarily to overthrow their oppressors. The second stage calls for ambushes and hit-and-run raids against enemy outposts; as the enemy is forced to spread his forces out, popular support for the revolution grows among the people, and conditions will eventually allow the rebels to move to the third stage, which is open conventional warfare and the overthrow of the oppressor.

Ho Chi Minh received some American support for the overriding fight against the Japanese. His guerrilla war was moderately successful, but in March 1941 the Japanese formally took over control of Indochina and forced French forces to leave. After the Japanese defeat, Ho Chi Minh declared the independence of the Democratic Republic of Vietnam and tried to prevent the French return.

But the French did return, and after some frustrating negotiations, Ho Chi Minh returned to the mountains and his guerrilla war. He had little success until 1949, when Mao Tse-tung established a Communist State in China. Thereafter, he received modern equipment and training for his troops from the experienced Chinese Communists.

The war with French colonial forces soon became serious, and both sides suffered punishing defeats. The French felt they had superior firepower if they could ever force the Viet Minh to stand and fight, but their inability to deal a crushing blow to the supposedly backward Communist forces was both frustrating and humiliating.

General Navarre was appointed Commander of French Forces in Indochina in 1953, and decided to implement a new strategy that he felt would lead to a convincing defeat of the Viet Minh. He planned to entice their main force units into set-piece battles—once committed, he would use superior French artillery, airpower and firepower to crush them. The first such confrontation was to occur near the village of Dien Bien Phu, which lies in a valley some 30 kilometers east of Laos, 120 kilometers south of China and 300 kilometers west of Hanoi.

The plan was to establish a major French base of operations, complete with airfield, at Dien Bien Phu. Attacks would then be launched against Viet Minh supply lines known to criss-cross the area, hoping to lure the enemy into a major attack on the heavily fortified French positions. But this concept was fatally flawed by several assumptions that were to result in catastrophe for the French: they did not believe the Viet Minh would be able to marshal a well-equipped, well-disciplined army many times the size of the French garrison in the area; they did not realize the Viet Minh would be able to position superior artillery and major anti-aircraft weapons in the heavily jungled hills of the area; and they relied far too heavily on their ability to resupply and support an isolated military force by air.

On 20 November 1953, all 65 C-47 cargo planes the French had in Indochina were used to drop three battalions of 2100 paratroopers in the area. They immediately set to work building defensive positions and improving the small airstrip. Within a week more than 4500 French troops were in the valley of Dien Bien Phu, and they began building strongpoints as an outer ring of defenses (supposedly named after girlfriends of one of the French commanders, but alphabetically sequential): Anne-Marie, Beatrice, Claudine, Dominique, Elaine, Francoise, Gabrielle, Huguette and, farther to the south and relatively isolated, Isabelle.

The valley of Dien Bien Phu was recognized by both sides as a key position for control over the flow of Viet Minh supplies. At the time of the French arrival in November, the 148th Regiment of the Viet Minh Army was in the surrounding hills; nearby was the 316th Division, consisting of three infantry regiments and an artillery regiment. Giap was cautious, however, and refrained from attacking until he could build his numerical superiority to overwhelming proportions. To that end, he sent the 304th and the 308th Divisions from the Red River Delta region to the Dien Bien Phu area to assist in a major attack on the French outpost.

French intelligence learned of this, and General Navarre visited and inspected the positions at Dien Bien Phu. On 3 December 1953, he issued a directive that the main headquarters at Dien Bien Phu and the airstrip be held at all costs, even if some of the outlying strongpoints had to be given up to reinforce the main garrison. Resupplies and reinforcements would be landed on the airstrip, from which casualties could be evacuated. More French troops were flown into Dien Bien Phu, but their force would obviously be far outnumbered by the Viet Minh force gathering for the attack; apparently, the threat of their artillery or anti-aircraft capability was not treated seriously.

French patrols began raiding out from Dien Bien Phu in December, but by the end of January, Viet Minh ambushes restricted them to the valley of their base. By early February, the entire valley was ringed by Viet Minh troops, and the only serviceable road, Route 41, was blocked. The first artillery fire from fixed Viet Minh positions hit the airstrip about that time, and anti-aircraft fire was directed against French aircraft using it. French patrols were being hit hard, and by the middle of February, their casualties since November had exceeded 1000 men. Reinforcements were rushed in, but the anti-aircraft fire was increasingly effective; resupplies were now coming in largely by parachute as a result. But still the main Viet Minh attack was not launched, as Communist troops gathered in the surrounding hills.

The French positions were manned by a polyglot of colonial troops (Vietnamese, Laotians, Moroccans, Algerians and other Africans), Foreign Legionnaires (predominantly Germans, Italians, Spaniards and Eastern Europeans) and elite French paratroops and commandos. By 12 March, when it was clear that Giap was about to attack, the French had 11,000 troops on the ground. They would receive 4000 reinforcements as the battle progressed. They were supported by 24 105mm medium howitzers, four 155mm heavy howitzers, 24 heavy mortars and ten tanks.

The Viet Minh were to use upward of 64,000 troops in their siege, equipped with more than 100 105mm howitzers, 50 75mm howitzers, 30 heavy mortars, 50 37mm Russian anti-aircraft guns and numerous 106mm recoilless rifles and Russian rocket launchers.

On 13 March the Viet Minh launched their attack with heavy artillery and mortar bombardments of the airstrip and Strongpoints Gabrielle and Beatrice to the north. The Viet Minh artillery fire from concealed positions was withering, and counterbattery fire by the French did little to affect it. Human-wave attacks on Gabrielle and Beatrice ensued, and masses of Viet Minh bodies, victims of mines and small-arms fire, surrounded the barbed wire defenses. Beatrice fell quickly, its defenders trapped by the attacking hordes. Gabrielle had been considered the least vulnerable of the strongpoints, with more defenders and armament than any other. But the artillery attack was ferocious: although the first masses of Viet Minh infantrymen throwing themselves on the wire were killed, the seemingly endless waves that followed were unstoppable. A counterattack launched from the central Dien

Bien Phu sector by French infantry with tank support was stopped, and surviving defenders at Gabrielle were forced to retreat to nearby Strongpoints Anne-Marie and Huguette.

The French suffered 1500 casualties in losing Strongpoints Gabrielle and Beatrice, but the Viet Minh had suffered thousands more. Still, Giap's willingness to send hordes of Viet Minh soldiers to certain death on the barbed wire in order to take those positions must have had a staggering impact on the French defenders. And Giap could continuously and freely feed reinforcements to the defenders' guns, while the French ability to resupply remaining positions was increasingly tenuous.

On 23 March Strongpoint Anne-Marie fell to a similar attack. The Viet Minh tightened their ring around the remaining French strongpoints and the central fortifications and airstrip, cutting off Isabelle to the south, whose defenders were fighting fiercely. But Communist forces were relentless in their indifference to losses.

The Viet Minh next concentrated their effort against the strongpoints east and south of the airstrip known as 'the Hills.' The French felt that these positions were crucial for their survival, given their command of the region. Again, massive artillery barrages preceded human-wave attacks. The French were driven back, but in a ferocious counterattack managed to retake two of their strongpoints. Meanwhile, a column from Isabelle that attempted to reach the central-headquarters position was driven back. No further contact would be made with that isolated enclave, although it would not fall to the Viet Minh until the very end.

On 1 April Giap arrived on the field to take personal command of his troops. The French had suffered some 2000 casualties in defending the Hills, but mounted a strong counterattack against Viet Minh forces around Huguette to the north. This relieved much of the pressure, French reinforcements were parachuted in and morale picked up.

With new life, the French counterattacked the Hills on 10 April. The Viet Minh reacted with additional sacrifices, but were unable to stop the determined French. For the first time, Giap began to consider his tactics of launching human-wave attacks without concern for his casualties, which were by now well over 20,000. He reoriented his operation, concentrating on more conventional siege tactics that included the laborious digging of trenches and bunkers. The Viet Minh redirected their efforts, giving the French defenders a welcome respite as they tightened the noose.

The Viet Minh had been able to bring superior forces to bear against the French, including cumbersome artillery and anti-aircraft weapons, as a function of pure human will. Their movement and logistical supply was made possible by raw courage alone, as an army with ant-like tenacity forced howitzers and other cumbersome materiel through thick jungle and up forbidding hills.

The heat of battle cooled several degrees, as Giap settled in to squeeze the life out of the French. Meanwhile, the French Government was scrambling for allied support. On 24 April the French asked the US Government to launch B-29 bombing raids against the Communist positions at Dien Bien Phu. It was hoped that such strikes would break the siege, forcing the Viet Minh to withdraw and allowing the French to reinforce their garrison. The French found considerable support for their request in powerful American political circles, but after less than a week of discussion, the US refused. The American Government, just ending an inconclusive war against Communist forces in Korea, would have seemed ready to lend support to another fight against international Communism, especially on behalf of a long-standing ally like France. But it appears the telling factor that kept American forces out of Indochina at this time was the oppressive colonial nature of the French presence in Indochina, a system that flew in the face of American tradition.

Two other plans were being developed by the French Government in last-ditch efforts to stave off the humiliation of an overwhelming defeat. The first, code-named Operation Condor, proposed that a relief column of French troops move overland from Laos, hook up with another contingent of paratroopers transported to their locations by air from Hanoi, and break through to rescue the remnants of the Dien Bien Phu garrison. While it was realized that American bomber strikes would greatly increase the chances of success for Operation Condor, the decisions on its implementation were intentionally made independent of US support. When the requested bombing support was denied, Operation Condor was still hurriedly launched, although with dramatically lessened expectations of saving the day for Dien Bien Phu.

The other plan, Operation Albatross, called for a desperate break-out by the remnants of the French garrison; in the event, the French simply did not have the aerial resources to support such a move. In any case, French soldiers in place were unwilling to abandon their thousands of wounded compatriots to the Viet Minh.

By 1 May the size of the French perimeter had been reduced from an original 50 kilometers to less than eight. The Viet Minh now held virtually all the high ground, where they emplaced massive artillery and rained down death. Giap had been able to freely evacuate his wounded and dead and replace them with fresh troops, totaling over 60,000 as the end drew near. The French garrison was reduced to the point where there were no more than 8000 effective combat troops defending their emplacements surrounded by thousands of dead and wounded. The air was heavy with the stench of death.

Ammunition, food and reinforcements continued to arrive by parachute, but virtually everyone recognized at this point that it was a lost cause. Viet Minh anti-aircraft fire caused the drops to be made from much higher altitudes than had previously been the case, and Viet Minh trenches ran right up to the edge of French defenses: thus, many of the parachutes drifted down into Communist hands. The French had lost the use of over half their artillery pieces and mortars, and small-arms ammunition was desperately low.

On 1 May the Viet Minh began a final crushing barrage of artillery and mortar shells on the French positions. Unknown to the French, the Communist forces had also been digging tunnels under French strongpoints, which they filled with explosives in anticipation of the final assault.

That assault was launched on 6 May. The preceding artillery and mortar barrage was followed by fresh human-wave attacks on the barbed wire as the tunnels were blown by remote control. But not all the tunnels had been accurately placed, and the result was to slow the attackers considerably and increase the number who fell to French fire. French air strikes were increasingly useless: from the pilot's seat, attacking Viet Minh infantry soon became inseparable from the French defenders. Great personal heroism was shown by the French troops in many locations, particularly by the paratroopers and the Foreign Legionnaires. But Viet Minh reinforcements seemed unending, and while many positions refused to surrender, all were eventually taken.

The French commander on the ground, General De Castries, did not yield his central control point at Dien Bien Phu until all other French defenders had been killed or captured. That finally occurred at 5:30 PM on 7 May 1954. When news of the capitulation reached the last strongpoint at Isabelle a few moments later, that outpost, too, surrendered. At the time Isabelle was taken, the Operation Condor forces from Laos had it in sight, though there had been no chance of reaching it in time to change the outcome.

The battle for Dien Bien Phu, which had lasted for 56 days, was over. During the early part of the siege, some wounded had been flown out, but as the use of the airstrip was increasingly restricted by hostile fire, they had been kept in makeshift hospitals and aid stations, or later simply in whatever shelter could be found. The original contingent of 11,000 troops had been reinforced by some 4000 who arrived by plane or parachute. When the Viet Minh finally overran the French positions, the French had suffered 2200 killed and over 6000 wounded. More than 6000 unwounded French soldiers were taken prisoner, but fewer than half those captured survived prison camp.

The French had dropped an average of just over 100 tons of supplies by parachute on the French garrison each day while it was besieged. While the Viet Minh had no aircraft of their own, their anti-aircraft and artillery fire had heavily damaged French resources and made the airstrip virtually unusable.

It is difficult to estimate Viet Minh casualties, although it is clear that they lost well over 10,000 killed and 20,000 wounded during the battle. The early stages, when Giap ordered human-wave attacks without regard to loss, were especially costly to them. When he later changed tactics and began to concentrate on trench warfare, his casualties were dramatically reduced, but so were the speed and psychological impact of his battlefield successes.

Even today, military analyses of this battle vary, with opinions ranging from those who say the outcome was obvious from the first day to those who argue that it was a very near thing. In any case, since it is always the losers who look for explanations, most observers agree on several items: major French shortcomings are seen in their underestimation of the size, armament and capability of Viet Minh forces, and in their overestimation of both their ability to resupply the garrison via cargo aircraft and the effectiveness of their fighters, fighter bombers, and artillery against massed infantry, particularly when sheltered by trenchworks.

Some fifteen years later, the same duet would be danced again, with Western troops defending an isolated outpost against a far larger Vietnamese Communist force of attackers, this time at a place called Khe Sanh. The only major differences would be the far greater availability to the US of cargo and tactical aircraft, as well as supporting artillery, but these factors would be enough to reverse the outcome.

CHOPPER WAR

Battle of the Ia Drang Valley

After the French agreed to withdraw from Indochina, Vietnam was divided, in keeping with the Geneva Accords, into a Communist-controlled state in the North, and a non-Communist state in the South. The population of this Southern state was swollen by nearly a million anti-Communist refugees who streamed down from the North in 1954 and 1955; only tens of thousands moved in the opposite direction. Although the Geneva Accords specified that the division of Vietnam was temporary and would be ended by an election in 1956, bitter hostility between the two political camps quickly destroyed any possibility that such an election would actually take place.

During the late 1950s, a Communist revolution was begun in South Vietnam by a trained cadre of former Viet Minh soldiers who had stayed behind: they became known as the Viet Cong. This group repudiated the new anti-Communist government in South Vietnam as a group of opportunists who had been closely tied to the French, while the Communist leader Ho Chi Minh was painted as a patriotic nationalist who had led the fight against French control.

This xenophobic call swayed many uneducated Vietnamese who knew nothing of the reality of life under Communism. By 1959 the Viet Cong in South Vietnam were being assisted in their efforts by major units of the North Vietnamese regular army. Common tactics of Communist forces to further this cause included murder, kidnapping, impressment and other acts of terrorism against the civilian population. The result of this carrot-stick approach, given the instability of the South Vietnamese military and the ineffectiveness of their government, was that large sections of the country began to fall under Communist control.

The US Government was alarmed, and to preclude the collapse of nascent freedom, sent growing numbers of American military advisers to train and assist the troops of South Vietnam. From a few hundred during the 1950s, the US military presence grew to 3000 in 1961, 11,000 in 1962, 16,000 in 1963 and 23,000 in 1964. By 1965, however, Communist pressure had increased to the point that the country's survival was severely threatened, and American combat units were sent into the fight.

One of the first American divisions to arrive in the summer of 1965 was the 1st Cavalry (Airmobile)—with state-of-the-art technology. Well trained in the Airmobile mode, it derived enormous flexibility from heavy use of the helicopters with which it was equipped. Deployed in the sparsely populated, jungle-covered mountains of the Central Highlands, the 1st Cav covered areas dramatically larger than could conventional infantry. Operations were coordinated with those of elite Special Forces, or 'Green Berets.' These were highly trained US officers and non-commissioned officers who played a special role in the Vietnam War: they lived under primitive conditions in the Central Highlands, with the ethnic minority groups known as Montagnards, forming Civilian Irregular Defense Group (CIDG) forces with which to fight the Communists. Operating from a secure mountain camp with a well-armed CIDG force of hundreds, a few Green Berets could range with impunity over large areas of mountainous terrain, providing valuable intelligence, raising havoc with North Vietnamese communication lines and 'safe' areas, ambushing reinforcements and destroying or capturing supplies. There were many of these camps, and the Special Forces soon became a major problem for the Communists.

The North Vietnamese commander in the Western Highlands area, General Chu Huy Man, had decided to launch major attacks in the fall of 1965 against American Special Forces camps and the city of Pleiku. He had at his disposal the 32nd, 33rd and 66th North Vietnamese Army Regiments, each roughly the size of an American brigade of three battalions. His plans were to be interrupted by the sudden arrival on the scene of the 1st Cav, whose main base was established at An Khe, some 70 kilometers from the coast. They soon began conducting strong patrols as far as the Ia Drang Valley, another 100 km west and only 20km short of the Cambodian border. They were moving rapidly in their helicopters, seeking to find, fix and destroy North Vietnamese forces. In early November, the 3rd Brigade of the 1st Cav assumed responsibility for the Ia Drang Valley: it was here that General Man would hurl all his forces against them in an unsuccessful attempt to overrun and destroy them. The battle was a classic confrontation between airmobile American troops and perhaps six to eight times their number of the best North Vietnamese soldiers.

American intelligence showed the Ia Drang Valley to be a major enemy staging area, with at least one North Vietnamese regiment using it as their major base. On 10 November General Man decided to launch an attack on 16 November by his three regiments against the Plei Mei Special Forces camp. He had attacked it earlier with only his 33rd Regiment, and had been driven off with great losses. This time he would take no chances and directed that the new attack be launched from a staging area at the foot of Chu Pong Mountain in the Ia Drang Valley.

Meanwhile, also on 10 November, General Harry Kinnard, the Commander of the 1st Cav, had directed Colonel Thomas Brown, commander of his 3rd Brigade, to sweep the heavily wooded region south of the Ia Drang River that covered the base of Chu Pong Mountain. Next day the 33rd NVA regiment was establishing itself in the valley between Chu Pong and Ia Drang, reorganizing and absorbing reinforcements after its disastrous losses in the attack on Plei Mei. The three battalions of the 66th NVA Regiment, newly arrived from the north, were located on both sides of the Ia Drang, a few kilometers to the west, while the 32nd NVA Regiment was another 10km farther west, on the northern bank of the Ia Drang. General Man had intended to buttress his force with a battalion each of 120mm mortars and 14.5mm twin-barrel anti-aircraft guns for the renewed attack on Plei Mei, but both units were still moving south on the Ho Chi Minh Trail at the time, and the attack would have to await their arrival.

The evening of 13 November, Colonel Brown met with the commander of the 1st Battalion, 7th Cavalry, Lt Colonel Harold Moore, and told him to conduct an airmobile assault into the Ia Drang Valley near the base of Chu Pong the next morning, and to follow the assault with search-and-destroy foot patrols in the area through 15 November. Moore's troops were just south of Plei Mei at the time, so the move would not take long. Fire support for the operation was to be provided by two 105mm howitzer batteries located at Landing Zone Falcon, east of the target area.

Moore alerted his company commanders to assemble their troops for movement, with an attack order to be issued at 0830, when the first heliborne assaults would begin. Before that time, he planned to conduct thorough reconnaissance flights over the area and finalize his plans. There were only three open clearings large enough to serve as landing zones in the area, codenamed Tango, Yankee and X-Ray. Malaria and administrative considerations combined meant that his companies would be at two-thirds of their authorized strength for the assault—about 150 men each. Also, in the few months they had been in Vietnam, no American units had as yet tied into major North Vietnamese units for a prolonged fight, and it looked like the Ia Drang Valley might be the place where this would change. Consequently, Moore decided to land all four companies on the same LZ and keep them within mutually supportive distance as they conducted their search.

First light on 14 November saw reconnaissance helicopters dashing through the Ia Drang Valley and around the base of Chu Pong. Colonel Moore quickly decided that X-Ray was the best location for the assault, but the reconnaissance flights had surely alerted the enemy, so artillery preparation fire would be directed on all three areas beforehand. The latest intelligence showed an enemy battalion slightly northwest of X-Ray, and a force of undetermined size to the southwest.

By 1030 hours, Company B of the 1st Bn, 7th Cavalry was landing unopposed at X-Ray, Lt Colonel Moore among them. As the helicopters began to ferry the rest of the battalion forward, the first foot-reconnaissance patrols from X-Ray met no resistance. Then a North Vietnamese deserter was captured, who told them there were many North Vietnamese troops on Chu Pong, eager to fight Americans. At dawn that morning, elements of the NVA forces scheduled to attack Plei Mei on the 16th had left their staging areas to move into position to the east. But when General Man learned of the landings at X-Ray in late morning, he immediately changed plans: the 66th and 33rd Regiments would attack and destroy the American troops; Ple Mei could wait. By noon most of the 66th and 33rd were poised at the base of Chu Pong to assault X-Ray.

As A Company arrived at X-Ray by helicopter, Moore ordered B Company to move to the west toward Chu Pong. After crossing a dry creek bed, B Company fanned out with two platoons abreast, a third in reserve with Captain Herren, the company commander. They began moving up a ridge toward Chu Pong through thick jungle, then became heavily engaged with superior enemy forces. Second Lieutenant Henry Herrick's platoon was quickly separated from the rest of the company and surrounded by North Vietnamese soldiers eager for the kill. Captain Herren tried to force his way to their rescue with his other platoons, but the enemy small-arms fire was devastating, and contact could not be re-established.

Meanwhile, back on X-Ray, the last helicopter loads of Company A troopers were arriving amid a hail of 60 and 81mm enemy mortar fire. Captain Ramon Nadal, the A Company Commander, sent Second Lieutenant Walter Marm forward with his platoon to assist B Company. Soon after he arrived in the B Company position, Lieutenant Marm noted enemy forces moving around to his left, toward X-Ray. A squad leader escorting a group of wounded back to X-Ray quickly reappeared with word that they were surrounded. The company-sized NVA unit moving to cut them off, however, made the mistake of trying to traverse the dry creek bed along which the rest of A Company was concealed. When they were well into the trap, A Company slaughtered them. C and D Companies were now arriving and securing X-Ray, and A Company moved rapidly forward and joined B Company. Both companies lined their men up and tried to move up the ridge to the rescue of Lt Herrick's platoon, but they were met by an enormous volume of enemy fire that stopped them cold. In spite of air and artillery support, the Americans had their hands full, the fighting often a ferocious hand-to-hand struggle for survival. Lieutenant Marm at one point assaulted a machine-gun position, killing enemy soldiers with hand grenades and his M-16 before he was shot in the face. Although Marm later received a Medal of Honor for his actions, the two-company assault was unable to reach Lt Herrick.

As evening fell, Lt Colonel Moore ordered A and B Companies back to X-Ray. C and D Companies were heavily involved there fending off enemy attacks, and while Moore disliked having to stop the rescue mission, it appeared the enemy was intent on overruning X-Ray and destroying the whole battalion. He would mount another rescue effort in the morning, but if the enemy discovered how A and B Companies were strung out, the whole battalion might be destroyed piecemeal.

The surrounded platoon was hard pressed. The 27-man unit had suffered eight killed, including Lt Herrick and the second in command, Sergeant Palmer; one of the squad leaders, Sergeant Savage, took command. With expertly placed artillery barrages added to small-arms fire from the survivors, he managed to stave off three major enemy attacks during the night.

When A and B Companies arrived back at X-Ray, they quickly slipped into their perimeter-defense positions. B Company from the 2nd Battalion, 7th Cavalry, had also arrived as reinforcement, but enemy fire against X-Ray made it impossible for any more reinforcements to land. Colonel Brown had directed the remainder of the 2nd of the 7th to Landing Zone Macon, ten kilometers north of X-Ray, and sent the 2nd Battalion of the 5th Cavalry to Landing Zone Victor, three kilometers southeast. He directed the 2nd of the 5th to move on foot to reinforce Moore's battalion the next morning.

That night, the 8th Battalion of the 66th NVA Regiment was moved into the area and charged with attacking the eastern side of the X-Ray perimeter, which would be defended by Company D, 1st of the 7th. General Man also acquired control of the H-15 Main Force Viet Cong Battalion and threw it against the south side of X-Ray, defended by Company C, 1st of the 7th. The 32nd Regiment had not been thrown into the fight, and the NVA heavy mortar and anti-aircraft guns were still on their way to X-Ray. All night long, the X-Ray perimeter was heavily probed, but the defenders were well entrenched; using tactical air missions as well as artillery, they prevented the enemy assault from overrunning American lines. The two artillery batteries at LZ Falcon fired over 4000 rounds that night, and they clearly swung the balance. While X-Ray received heavy mortar fire that night, and was laced with murderous small-arms tracers, the American soldiers were dug in and prepared, and the enormous volume of enemy fire did minimal damage.

At first light, enemy fire had ended. Lieutenant Colonel Moore directed company commanders to send small reconnaissance patrols out from their lines, and then meet at his position to discuss the rescue of the isolated platoon, still hanging on to the ridge. The patrol from C Company hit enemy resistance almost immediately, however, and soon the entire company front was under heavy fire. It was soon apparent that this was a serious attack, and despite punishing artillery and air support, North Vietnamese soldiers were reaching the Company C foxhole line. Lt Colonel Moore had few options, and ordered Company A to send a platoon to C's support. No sooner had the platoon been dispatched than Company D also came under a heavy ground attack that threatened to overwhelm them. Lt Colonel Moore commited his reserve, the battalion reconnaisance platoon, to Company D, then called Colonel Brown and asked for reinforcements.

The air support and artillery were both heavy and accurate

now, often falling right on the perimeter, but staving off the desperate assaults on Companies C and D. By 0800, a third attack had been launched by the enemy against Company A's position, and the fight for X-Ray was taxing the Americans to the limit. Lt Colonel Moore brought a platoon of B Company, 2nd of the 7th, to his command position at the center of X-Ray as a final reserve to throw into gaps that might appear. But the defenders held strong, and death rained down on the enemy in the form of artillery rounds and air-delivered bombs—including a B-52 strike on Chu Pong—as well as small-arms fire from the perimeter. At 0900 hours, in spite of fierce enemy fire, helicopters began to arrive at X-Ray with reinforcements from A Company, 2nd of the 7th Cav. Then the volume of American fire began to pay off, and the enemy assault first slackened, then ceased. The all-out North Vietnamese attempts to overrun the perimeter and destroy the 1st of the 7th Cav had failed.

Only three kilometers away, additional reinforcements were on the way. Having arrived at LZ Victor during the previous day and night, the 2nd Battalion, 5th Cavalry was moving on foot toward the sound of the guns. They soon met heavy resistance, and had to fight much of the way to X-Ray. There they linked up with the 1st of the 7th at the embattled perimeter by noon. Lt Colonel Tully, commander of the 2nd of the 5th, co-ordinated the next move with Lt Colonel Moore. Since they were fresh, A and C Companies of the 2nd of the 5th were committed to accompany B Company, 1st of the 7th, to rescue their isolated platoon, still clinging to the ridge under Sergeant Savage's command. Tully would accompany this rescue force, while Moore absorbed B Company, 2nd of the 5th, into his perimeter.

Tully started his move at 1300 hours, and met only sporadic resistance via sniper fire. Soon they reached the battered platoon, whose survival was largely attributable to Sergeant Savage's expert and timely use of artillery fire during the night. The task of transporting all the dead and wounded back to X-Ray proved arduous and time-consuming, but by 1600 hours the two-battalion perimeter was locked up tight.

During the early evening, the perimeter was subjected to

enemy probes and sniper fire, but no serious attacks were launched until after midnight: then a series of code whistles near B Company, 2nd of the 7th, alerted the defenders to a major attack. But this time there were several companies waiting, well dug in, as reserves, and the American defenders were secure and confident. Although this attack was massive and lasted much of the night, it came only in one small area, and four artillery batteries, plus all available mortars, were concentrated to blunt it effectively. Although many enemy soldiers fell as close as a few meters from American positions, they never overran them, and would get no closer. As the sun rose, the enemy fire drifted away, and the defenders were aghast at the carnage unveiled to them in the morning light.

The forces on the perimeter started the morning with a 'mad minute,'—every weapon fired on full automatic for 60 seconds. This action provoked fire from an enemy force a hundred meters or so distant, which was soon silenced by artillery fire. Each element on the perimeter sent reconnaissance patrols forward, but the only resistance fire was from wounded enemy soldiers. After a further saturation of the area by artillery, the companies conducted sweeps forward from their lines to a distance of some 500 meters. The American soldiers were stunned by what they saw and counted. During the several days of combat at X-Ray, the enemy had hurled major forces against the perimeter in an effort to overrun the American unit. They had failed, and while the hundreds of trails showed that many bodies had been dragged away, they counted 643 dead enemy soldiers on the field. The American casualties were 79 killed, 121 wounded and none missing.

The 1st Cav would continue to operate with freedom throughout the region for years to come, and would often engage major enemy units in prolonged fights. However, never again would the North Vietnamese hurl their forces against Cav positions with such utter abandon. If nothing else, they learned that lesson in the Ia Drang Valley.

MASSIVE POWER PUNISHES

Junction City

Much of American public attention in the Vietnam War was focused via the media on elite American units: the paratroopers of the 101st Airborne Division, the 'Green Berets' of the Special Forces, the Marines on the DMZ, or the Airmobile troops of the 1st Cav in the Central Highlands. This last unit in particular had daily access to helicopters for any movement, which gave their actions a certain flash and color that caught the public eye. But the great bulk of the war was fought by straight leg infantrymen, and while they may have been inserted into a particular area by helicopter, all their subsequent tactical movements were made on foot, unromantically slogging it out in the bush.

Any clear understanding of the Vietnam War must include a close look at the role played by 'Joe Footsoldier.' Only after the situation he dealt with in the field is understood can any greater insight into the larger picture of the war be gained. Operation 'Junction City' provides an excellent opportunity for a closeup view of this reality. To give an idea of the scale of military forces in this and other operations, the following facts are mentioned at the outset. For American, South Vietnamese, North Vietnamese and Viet Cong units involved in field operations, the individual soldier was usually organized into platoons of 20 to 40 men. Three to five platoons formed a company of anywhere from 80 to 150 men, and four to six companies constituted a battalion, whose strength was generally 400 to 800. Three to five battalions formed a brigade, a regiment, or a group (depending on the unit type) of 1500 to 4000, and three to five regiments or brigades together constituted a division of 5000 to 20,000 men. At the battalion, brigade, and division levels, the head-count strength was significantly supplemented by various support troops.

After their arrival in Vietnam in 1965, US divisions and separate brigades remained in specified areas, but Viet Cong and North Vietnamese units avoided major contact: American forces were unable to lure them into a setpiece battle. In late October of 1966, elements of the US 1st and 25th Infantry Divisions were seeking Communist units in War Zone C, an area some 50 by 80 kilometers sandwiched against the Cambodian border to the west and north, and some hundred kilometers north of Saigon. This had been a safe haven for Communist forces even under the French, and when both units almost simultaneously hit elements of the 9th Viet Cong Division, the American command threw in heavy reinforcements. Eventually, parts of the 1st, 4th and 25th US Infantry Division, as well as several South Vietnamese battalions—over 22,000 Allied troops—participated in the operations, heavily supported by air and artillery. By 29 November the enemy had left 1106 dead on the battlefield, but later intelligence reports showed that he listed 2130 killed—including over 1000 by airstrikes—almost 900 wounded and over 200 missing or captured. In addition, the Communist logistical system had been pillaged by American and South Vietnamese forces, hurting the enemy badly. Although this operation had begun almost by accident, it had succeeded in pinning down and destroying major Communist units. Hoping for more of the same, General Westmoreland directed that a major multi-division operation be launched against different sections of War Zone C in February of 1967.

So was born Operation Junction City. It was to be the largest operation to date, using 22 infantry battalions, 14 artillery battalions, 4 South Vietnamese battalions and tactical air support as required. The primary goal of Junction City was to locate and destroy the Central Office of South Vietnam

(COSVN), the administrative and logistical headquarters through which Hanoi managed the war in South Vietnam, and which was believed to be in the target area. The operation was further charged with destroying VC/NVA forces and installations, with building Special Forces camps, airstrips and roads and with repairing or installing bridges.

Junction City was planned with the utmost secrecy, and was scheduled to go through two phases. The first phase, from 22 February to 17 March, involved the deployment of elements of the 1st and 25th US Infantry Divisions, the 173rd Airborne Brigade, and South Vietnamese Ranger and Marine battalions in the shape of a giant horseshoe some 45 kilometers in perimeter. They would establish blocking positions in the north, east and west, while a brigade of the 25th plus the 11th Armored Cavalry Regiment would enter the southern opening of the horseshoe and drive north, hopefully pinning Communist forces against the waiting American units. The second phase, from 18 March until the middle of April, would involve basically the same American units conducting comparatively freeform search-and-destroy operations in an area of War Zone C east of the horseshoe phase. Brigades from the 4th and 9th Infantry Divisions would also participate in portions of Junction City, making it the strongest show of American military might to date. By its nature, it became a true showcase of America's greatest strengths—and weaknesses—in the Vietnam War.

In order to align the 1st and 25th Divisions so they could easily move to their Junction City blocking positions, two diversionary operations were launched the first week in February. Operation Gadsden involved two brigades of the 25th Division along the Cambodian border. During its 20-day duration, a series of airmobile assaults and attacks by heavy mechanized battalions encountered little resistance. Intelligence reports had predicted the presence of several Viet Cong and North Vietnamese regiments, as well as major supply, training and administrative centers; all these plus extensive fortifications and storage areas were found. But the enemy chose to abandon rather than defend them, so they were destroyed or evacuated to the American rear.

Operation Tucson was conducted some 50 kilometers to the east of Gadsden by two Brigades of the 1st Infantry Division. Again, intelligence reports showed this to be an enemy sanctuary with many base camps and caches of supplies and materiel. Airmobile inserts and armored attacks uncovered more than anticipated, but little enemy resistance. After destroying what they could, both American divisions moved to their blocking positions for Junction City.

Despite the multiplicity of American units, there were only two divisional commands in the first phase of Junction City: the 1st and the 25th. For this operation, the 1st Division was made up of two of its own brigades along with the 1st Brigade US 9th Infantry Division, the 173rd Airborne Brigade and two Vietnamese Ranger battalions. The 25th had only one of its own brigades, as well as the 3rd Brigade of the 4th Infantry Division, the 196th Light Infantry Brigade and the 11th Armored Cavalry Regiment. The 1st Division elements were responsible for blocking the eastern and northern portions of the 'horseshoe,' while the 25th was to cover the western portion and also conduct the sweep north from the open southern end.

D-Day for the operation was 22 February, and the forces were inserted into their blocking positions without incident. Nine infantry battalions reached their position by air assault, eight of them using helicopters and one parachutes. The latter jump—the first combat parachute assault by an American battalion since the Korean War—was made by the 2nd Battalion 503rd Infantry, 173rd Airborne Brigade and associated other elements. At the same time, the 25th Division moved its units into position on the western side of the horseshoe, and the 3rd Brigade of the 1st Division drove north up Provincial Route 4 to close off the target area. The 2nd Brigade of the 25th and the 11th Armored Cavalry Regiment were poised at the open southern end of the horseshoe, prepared to launch their sweep north the following morning.

The terrain that was to be cleared in Phase I of Junction City was primarily flat, often marshy, with vegetation ranging from thin forests with scattered open areas to heavy jungle. Most of the American positions on the northern and western sides of the horseshoe were located within 5 kilometers of the Cambodian border, a privileged sanctuary into which the Americans could not venture. In spite of the fact that some 27,000 Allied troops were being used to cordon off the area and trap COSVN, it was extremely difficult to establish a seal with sufficient troop density. The Americans and South Vietnamese sought to deny exfiltration routes to Communist forces thoroughly familiar with the dense jungle, but to do this, their blocking forces operated out of secure fire support bases. These established, and equipped with heavy artillery support, they sent their infantry units out on search-and-destroy missions and ambush patrols along likely exit routes from the horseshoe. American and South Vietnamese forces had neither the manpower nor the inclination to line their troops up shoulder-to-shoulder around the horseshoe area. Still, the heavy patroling with strong artillery and air support seemed capable of accomplishing the desired end.

But the reviews were mixed. By 2 March, the 'Hammer' portion of the operation had been completed, and the internal area of the horseshoe had been meticulously searched. During the rest of Phase I, the blocking forces conducted continuous search-and-destroy operations in their assigned areas. There were a number of small engagements involving units smaller than company size, but for the most part, the enemy refused to make contact. The action throughout Phase I took the form mainly of daily contacts with enemy forces of fewer than 10 men, who invariably tried to slip away after the first burst of fire, and the continual discovery of more and more base camps. However, two major battles were fought during the first phase of Junction City—one on 28 February, the other on 10 March—both near Prek Klok.

The first battle of Prek Klok occurred when a battalion of the NVA stumbled into an American unit on the morning of 28 February. The 1st Battalion 16th Infantry, 1st Infantry Division was assigned the mission, during Phase I of Operation Junction City, of securing a section of Route 4, the southeast boundary of the horseshoe. At 0800, Company B, 1st of the 16th, left their night perimeter and headed east on a search-and-destroy mission. Some 2500 meters to the east was the stream Prek Klok, but B Company would not get that far.

The terrain was heavily jungled, and the company snaked along in a column, pausing at intervals and clearing their flanks with patrols sent out in a clover-leaf pattern. Movement was deadly slow. Around ten-thirty, the lead platoon was taken under heavy fire by three or more machine guns. Then flanking fire was brought to bear on them from the south. The enemy was not dug in, only rather moving through the jungle like B Company, but heading west toward Route 4. It was a classic 'meeting engagement,' wherein opposing forces on the march run into each other.

B Company's Commander, Captain Ulm, quickly brought his other two platoons forward in support and established an arclike position as they were brought under fire from the northeast. An American battery of heavy 155mm artillery was in direct support: soon steel was raining through the jungle on the enemy. The hostile fire was intense, however, and B Company was truly pinned down. In addition to the artillery, tactical air strikes also began to have their effect.

Around one o'clock, movement was detected to the west, and Captain Ulm rushed elements of his unit to close that side of the perimeter. They had no sooner reached their positions than they were brought under intense automatic-weapons fire. They were surrounded. But artillery and air strikes were redirected to cover the western side of the perimeter as well, and an inferno of death and destruction soon surrounded the American position. By two o'clock, the fire fight had diminished to scattered sniper fire, and by three, enemy contact had ended. At two-thirty, another company had been landed by helicopter some six hundred meters away and soon linked up with B Company, while a third company followed a few hours later.

The battle had been brief but intense. B Company had suffered 25 dead and 28 wounded. A sweep of the battlefield that afternoon and another the next morning found 167 dead, plus many blood trails where scores of dead or wounded had been dragged away. Truly, the air and artillery support had stemmed the tide and broken the back of the enemy attack.

A wounded prisoner captured the next morning was an officer in the 2nd Battalion 101st North Vietnamese Army Regiment. It was this battalion that had stumbled into B Company and been mauled by American firepower.

The second battle of Prek Klok took place on 10 March, but it was very different from the first. The Communist forces launched an all-out attack, under cover of darkness, against an American fire support base defended by a battalion of mechanized infantry. The 2nd Battalion (mechanized), 2nd Infantry, minus one company, was securing the perimeter of Artillery Fire Support Base II on Route 4, again in the southeast corner of the horseshoe area, not far from the site of Prek Klok I. Inside the circular 'wagon train' perimeter were two artillery batteries and a detachment of US Army Engineers. The engineers were building an airstrip and a Special Forces camp at that location.

The perimeter of the fire base was protected by foxholes, manned by infantrymen as well as men from the artillery and engineer detachments. Every fifty meters or so was one of the Armored Personnel Carriers (armored tracked vehicles on which are mounted 50-caliber as well as 7.62-mm M-60 machine guns) and they were dug in. Fields of fire had been cleared before all the defensive positions, and as ambush patrols and listening posts left the perimeter that night, American forces felt secure and well prepared for any enemy attack.

At about ten o'clock, the enemy launched a heavy mortar attack on the fire base. Over the next thirty minutes, literally hundreds of 120mm, 82mm and 60mm shells fell on the American positions. Then, about 10:30, the enemy launched a ground attack with two battalions against defensive positions along the eastern sector of the fire base, positions manned by A Company, 2nd of the 2nd. But the Americans were well prepared. Artillery from nearby fire support bases, as well as that at Prek Klok itself, surrounded the perimeter with a wall of steel.

The attack against A Company on the east was intense, with recoilless-rifle and automatic-weapons fire crashing into their defensive positions. Three of A Company's Armored Personnel Carriers were hit by armor-piercing RPG2 (Rocket

Propelled Grenade) rounds, and one of them suffered a direct hit with a mortar round. But with massive air and artillery support, the defenses held.

Limited attacks were also launched from the northeast and southeast, and the enemy's secondary attack came from the southwest. But they only hurled themselves into the teeth of the American defenses, and failed in their vain efforts to break through. Over five thousand rounds of artillery were fired that night, and hundreds of tactical air strikes launched. After an hour of fierce fighting, the enemy attack was broken. It was early morning hours before the hostile fire had ceased, and with first light, reconnaissance patrols cleared the field of battle. The bodies of 197 enemy dead were recovered, and five wounded were captured, all members of two battalions of the 272nd Regiment, 9th Viet Cong Division. US losses were 3 killed and 38 wounded. Once again, the strength and impregnability of a well-prepared American defensive position was demonstrated.

At midnight on 17 March, Phase I of Operation Junction City officially ended. The enemy had left 835 bodies on the field of battle and lost enormous logistical supplies and facilities. However, with greater knowledge of the terrain, the Communists had been able to elude the massive American defensive positions and slip through their lines and into Cambodia almost at will. It was a case of heavy cavalry against light infantry: if they could ever be caught, they stood no chance against the much stronger American forces. But once again, the VC and NVA proved maddeningly elusive.

Phase II began on 18 March and lasted for 28 days. The same basic units that had participated in Phase I moved into the section of War Zone C due east of the previous horseshoe formation. There they conducted independent 'search-and-destroy' operations, and American efforts to pin down and destroy enemy units were somewhat more successful. During Phase II, the enemy left nearly 1900 dead on the field of battle, and the 9th Viet Cong Division was virtually eliminated as a viable force. Three major battles took place in Phase II, all launched by the enemy after careful and meticulous preparation; all were unsuccessful in their efforts to overrun American positions and resulted in enormous Viet

Cong losses of personnel. If the Communists had thought to this point that they could take on even much smaller American units and defeat them in conventional warfare, they learned here that if artillery and air support could be used against them, they would be brutalized.

The first of these battles took place on 19 March at an American fire support base near Ap Bau Bang. Fire Support Base 20 was located in a clearing just west of Highway 13. To the south was a rubber plantation, while the rest of the perimeter was surrounded by heavily wooded areas. A Troop, 3rd Squadron, 5th Cavalry defended the base with its 129 men, 6 tanks, 20 M-113 Armored Personnel Carriers and 3 4.2-inch mortar carriers. Inside the base was B Battery, 7th Battalion, 9th Artillery. It was a small fire base, and the cavalry troop defense was the usual 'wagon train' loose circle, well dug in.

One of the three platoons in A Troop was sent out to an ambush position some 1500 meters north of the fire base and was in place by full dark at six o'clock that evening. At 10:50 a Viet Cong probe began, when fifteen belled cattle were driven toward the perimeter from Highway 13 over a hundred meters away. This was followed by fire from a Communist 50-caliber machine gun, but return fire from the defensive positions brought only silence.

Half an hour after midnight, the main attack was launched, with enemy mortar shells, rockets, rifle grenades and recoil-less-rifle fire smashing into the perimeter defenses. Some 20 minutes after the mortar attack opened, the main attack came from the rubber plantation on the south and southwest, with a secondary attack from the north. Massed troops from the 273rd Viet Cong Regiment walked out of the trees, as mortar rounds struck tanks and armored personnel carriers. By 1:00 AM a 'Spooky' C-47 armed with miniguns was on station above, pouring murderous fire onto the attackers, and helicopter gunships were on their way. But the Viet Cong attackers were reaching the defensive positions and overrunning some of the personnel carriers, to the point that crews were firing rounds of antipersonnel canister at each other, killing the enemy troops as they swarmed over the armored vehicles.

The American platoon that had been lying in ambush to

the north came barreling back down Highway 13 soon after one in the morning and was thrown into the line on the southern side of the perimeter, now wavering under the fierce assault. Meanwhile, elements of two other Cavalry troops to the south were racing north up Highway 13 to the rescue. By two o'clock, two more platoons had arrived and joined the fray. The tide of the attack was turned and then repelled. The Americans rapidly solidified and resupplied their defenses, evacuating dead and wounded as they reinforced their positions.

At five in the morning, the last Viet Cong attack was launched against the southern defenses, but artillery and air strikes blunted it before it got near the perimeter. By first light, enemy forces had withdrawn and the last air strikes and artillery barrages followed their retreat. Reconnaissance patrols found 227 enemy bodies and uncounted blood trails. US losses were 3 killed and 63 wounded. Air strikes had delivered 29 tons of ordnance and almost 3000 artillery rounds had been fired in defense of Fire Support Base 20. The three battalions of the 273rd Regiment, 9th Viet Cong Division, had gone all out to overrun this small American position, but had failed.

Another fire support base, this one much larger than that at Ap Bau Bang, was to be established for Phase II of Junction City in a jungle clearing near Suoi Tre, in the middle of War Zone C and only ninety kilometers northwest of Saigon. On 19 March—the day of the Ap Bau Bang battle—US helicopters airlanded the 3rd Battalion of the 22nd Infantry and the 2nd Battalion of the 77th Artillery in the specified location. Commanders of these units were Lieutenant Colonels John A Bender and John W Vessey, Jr (Vessey would later reach four-star rank and become the Chairman of the Joint Chiefs of Staff). They did not expect much action at this new fire base, code-named 'Gold,' but their very arrival showed otherwise: five large command-detonated charges were blown by the Viet Cong as the first flight of helicopters arrived. Three helicopters were destroyed and six more damaged, with a total of 15 Americans killed in the incident and 28 wounded.

The 3rd of the 22nd established a defensive perimeter on

the landing zone and began to dig in. In the afternoon, the 2nd Battalion 12th Infantry arrived at Gold by helicopter and moved off to the northwest. On 20 March work on the fire base defenses progressed rapidly, which was fortunate for the occupants, who could not know they would be subjected to a major attack the next day.

On the morning of the 21st, the new fire base was inundated with enemy mortar shells. Some 650 rounds fell on Gold, keeping American heads down as the Viet Cong moved their forces in close for the ground assault. Machine guns and recoilless rifles joined the fire, as masses of Viet Cong moved out of the treeline and rushed the perimeter in 'human-wave' formation. By seven o'clock the VC had broken through the northeastern section of the perimeter and the reaction force from the artillery battalion was thrown into the breach. Artillery fire from neighboring bases was brought to bear, and air strikes hammered the line from which the attacks were launched.

At 7:50, the entire northeastern section of the perimeter had been overrun by VC human-wave attacks. Artillery batteries in the center of the fire base leveled their tubes and fired 'beehive' rounds (canisters filled with hundreds of metal darts) into the waves of enemy soldiers attacking the southeastern portion of the perimeter. By 8:40, the northeastern, eastern and southeastern sections of the perimeter had withdrawn to a hasty secondary defensive line, and the artillery guns began firing beehive rounds against the massed Communist soldiers hurling themselves into their lines. The northern, western and southern sectors were holding their own, but the Viet Cong were now attacking from all sides. Air and artillery support were effective, but the enemy was everywhere. By 8:50 the artillery pieces on Fire Base Gold had exhausted their supply of beehive rounds and were firing high-explosive rounds into the enemy ranks at point-blank range.

Meanwhile, the 2nd Battalion 12th Infantry, which had landed at Gold on the 20th, was returning to the fire base's support. The defenses were still holding when the 2nd of the 12th broke through at 9 o'clock from the northwest and added their support to the beleaguered defenders. With this added force, the enemy on the east was driven back and the defenses on the original perimeter were regained. Two other battalions, one of mechanized infantry and one of tanks, were also rushing to the rescue from the south.

At 9:15, their vehicles came bursting out of the jungle, ripping into the massed enemy attackers from the rear. The carnage they beheld was frightful, and surviving enemy soldiers soon began to withdraw. By 9:30 the entire original perimeter was regained. Enemy fire faded away as defeated soldiers fled the field, dragging as many dead and wounded with them as they could.

By 10:30 the battle was over, with air and artillery strikes pursuing the retreating enemy. Truly, the Communists had paid a frightful price: they lost 647 men but had failed to take Fire Base Gold. American casualties were 31 dead and 109 wounded. Documents recovered from enemy dead showed that this abortive attack had been carefully planned and launched by the entire 272nd Regiment of the 9th VC Division and U-80 Artillery.

More than a week later, the third major battle of Junction City, Phase II, took place. On 30 March the 1st Battalion 26th Infantry was landed by helicopter in an open field surrounded by jungle, where they were to establish Fire Support Base George. Fierce enemy resistance was expected, since this was a major base camp area only five kilometers from the Cambodian border, but that first day brought no hostile fire or other contact. On 31 March the 1st Battalion 2nd Infantry landed at George, then moved two kilometers to the southwest, where they established their own position. The 1st of the 26th began an intensive search-and-destroy operation in the area, and although there were many signs of Communist forces, they seemed unwilling to fight.

Shortly after noon, major contact was made to the north of the landing zone by the reconnaissance platoon. The Americans were quickly pinned down by an estimated enemy battalion, and B Company moved to their rescue. The battalion commander of the 1st of the 26th was Lieutenant Colonel Alexander M Haig (who would also rise to four-star rank and later serve as US Secretary of State). As he sent B Company to rescue the reconnaissance team, he flew overhead in his 'command and control' helicopter. B Company was soon pinned down by heavy machine-gun fire, mortars, rockets and recoilless rifles; they were unable to control the situation. Col Haig called for artillery and air support, ordered his A Company forward, then landed and joined the B Company commander in the thick of the fray.

A Company soon arrived, but the Communist forces were far superior in numbers: they ripped and clawed at the Americans who were trying to break contact and pull back to their prepared defenses at Fire Base George. With massive intervention by artillery and air strikes, they were finally able to do this by five o'clock in the evening. American casualties from this firefight were 7 killed and 28 wounded.

Meanwhile, another infantry battalion, the 1st of the 16th, had landed at George to support the 1st of the 26th. The two battalions co-ordinated their defensive plans and locked into neighboring positions for the night. At five in the morning on 1 April, literally hundreds of 60mm, 82mm, and 120mm mortar rounds smashed into Fire Support Base George. Because of the strength of the defensive positions, however, only 12 men were wounded by this mortar barrage, which lasted some 20 minutes. As soon as it ended, the Viet Cong launched a major ground attack against the northeast edge of the perimeter. Three bunkers were quickly captured by the enemy, as they forced a penetration of the American defenses some hundred meters wide and forty meters deep. Desperate hand-to-hand fighting raged in the dark as the reconnaissance platoon was rushed into the breach in C Company's defenses. Intense artillery fire and massive air strikes were massacring Communist forces all around the fire base, and eventually this support had its effect. By 6:30 Communist penetrations had been stopped. More attacks hit the western and eastern sides of the perimeter, but were unable to make any headway under the heavy fire.

A massive counterattack was launched against the major intrusion into the northeast section of the landing zone, and by eight o'clock, the original defensive perimeter had been restored. Artillery and air strikes followed the enemy soldiers.

An immediate body count in the landing-zone clearing revealed 491 enemy soldiers. A more detailed sweep of the battlefield area later that day brought the total of enemy killed in the action to 609, plus an unknown number who were dragged away or died later from their wounds. The enemy units had been all three battalions of the 271st Regiment of the 9th Viet Cong Division and two battalions of the 70th Guard Regiment. US casualties were 17 killed and 102 wounded. The enemy forces had been thoroughly crushed in their unsuccessful attempts to take Fire Base George and driven in disarray from the field of battle.

This was to be the last major action in Operation Junction City. Of the five battles, four were initiated by the enemy in vain attempts to overrun American bases, while the other had been an accidental meeting engagement that was soon broken off by the numerically superior enemy. While all the enemy attacks were unsuccessful and cost him heavily in personnel, the major American goal of engaging and destroying or capturing large enemy forces in a US-engineered trap had failed. While it is true that enormous supplies of enemy materiel were captured in this operation, the VC and NVA were willing to meet in battle only on occasions and under circumstances of their choosing. Although on several occasions their forces were decimated by air and artillery in their all-out efforts to take American fire bases, these actions had been initiated by the Communists: when their attacks failed, they simply faded into the bush and disappeared into Cambodia. The analogy of trying to kill a mosquito with a sledge hammer is not inappropriate. But the mosquito certainly learned in the process not to try to bite a sledge hammer, nor to operate in the open where it could be quickly crushed or captured.

THE AIR WAR

As US military involvement in Vietnam increased during the 1960s, American air power began to play an increasingly important role in the conduct of the war. This was a natural enough occurrence, of course, for as a super-power stooping to conquer in the Third World, the United States sought to apply whatever technological advantages were available to resolve matters quickly in its favor.

In 1415, the English had introduced the longbow to the battlefield and used it to defeat a numerically superior French army at the battle of Agincourt. Since that time, man has continually sought to distance himself from the destruction he wreaks, to depersonalize and at the same time magnify the damage he could inflict at long range. The airplane was a perfect vehicle for such evolution, as demonstrated by the enormously successful bombing campaigns of World War II and Korea. Close attention continued to be focussed on developments of the military air arm, and by the middle 1960s, the air combat capabilities available to the US Government were far more sophisticated and deadly than anything seen in the past.

So it was that President Johnson responded to the 1964 North Vietnamese torpedo-boat attacks on US destroyers in the Gulf of Tonkin with air raids on North Vietnamese military bases. At this point, most American leaders truly believed that the death and destruction resulting from such raids would make the North Vietnamese pause and reconsider their actions. They were destined, however, to receive a lot of harsh education from the North Vietnamese on commitment to purpose. The air war touched on most of the American military presence in Indochina. Quite often, purely logistical and sometimes mundane tasks were performed by aircraft, ranging from transportation of troops and supplies to extraction of wounded soldiers from the field to reconnaissance photography from high altitudes. But for the sake of brevity, we will here concentrate on the use of airpower as a weapon to assist friendly ground forces, to punish their Communist adversaries, or to interdict Communist presence in or movement through a given area.

In February 1965, several Communist attacks against military barracks in South Vietnam resulted in the deaths of 31 American Advisors. President Johnson responded by sending 50 aircraft from US Navy carriers at Yankee Station in the Tonkin Gulf to strike North Vietnamese Army (NVA) barracks in Dong Hoi; additional Air Force and Navy aircraft later struck NVA barracks at Chanh Hoa and Vit Thu Lu. The precedent had been set, and the act of punishing the Communists by bombing North Vietnam became an almost automatic reaction.

Soon after the US Marines first landed in Danang in March 1965, a squadron of their F-4s immediately began flying close air-support missions. The US Air Force also began to arrive in strength that year, and by January 1966 had over 500 aircraft and 21,000 men on the ground at eight air bases in South Vietnam. As American ground forces began to take on North Vietnamese and Viet Cong units in earnest, it wasn't long before their powerful air arm was only a radio call away.

Previous American experience with air power in support of ground operations, however, had been in a conventional war context, and the attempts to transfer such tactics to what was quite often little more than a guerrilla war were not always successful. Although the use of tactical air support by ground troops was made more effective as individual experience of both pilots and ground commanders grew, the very nature of such use was burdened by an unfortunate inherent flaw. The attitude of the aircraft commanders was that they were there to serve the men on the ground, that unlimited expenditures of ordnance would be made without question when so requested by the ground commander. The underlying thought was that no price was too high to pay to save the life of even one American soldier. While this attitude was understandable, it was often unknowingly abused, for to the soldiers on the ground, air assets were 'free,' and there was an unending supply of aircraft and ordnance available to them just for the asking.

Too often, the unwritten rule became never to waste the opportunity, however strained, to use tactical air-support firepower. This was reinforced by standard operating procedure for Air Force and Navy fighter-bombers: once they had taken off with a load of bombs, they would have to drop them before they returned to their bases. This meant that if they were diverted from their primary targets, for whatever reason, they would then go to secondary or tertiary targets to drop their ordnance. Often, such targets had been arbitrarily picked on a map as 'likely avenues' for Communist movement. That meant that, among the many hundreds of thousands of tons of bombs expended by American aircraft in Vietnam, a disturbing proportion was simply thrown away on jungled hillsides where human feet had never trod. Aside from the sheer waste involved, this sponsored a blindness on the part of many American soldiers to the fact that, quite often, a flight of F-4s or even B-52s was not the best weapon to use against a squad of light infantrymen out there in the woods: sometimes you just have to go out there and fight them yourself.

Once US Air Force units were on the ground in South Vietnam, though, tactical air support was always readily available, and it was often hard to value things fairly. In addition, US Navy aircraft carriers were poised at Dixie Station off the coast of South Vietnam and Yankee Station in the Tonkin Gulf. A silent competition for the most and the best wartime air combat experiences quickly sprang up between these two services and lasted in all geographic theaters of operation for the duration of the war. But Congress could never be faulted for frugality in the provision of supporting weaponry or ordnance of every kind, and US tactical air support in the Vietnam War was truly lavish.

In January 1966, the US Marines in I Corps were entangled with a number of North Vietnamese units, and many Air Force, Navy and Marine fliers got their first taste of combat. Thereafter, the war became a daily (or nightly) routine of dropping bombs: whenever a US unit made contact with Communist forces, the skies were soon swarming with aircraft. The war to that point had been tilting in favor of the Communists, but the arrival of American troops, backed by massive air and artillery support, had a major impact, and by late 1966 the tables were turning.

The only major North Vietnamese military success in 1966 occurred in March, when, after a long battle, they overran a US Special Forces camp in the A Shau Valley near the Laotian border. During the fight for that camp, one American propeller-driven A-1E Skyraider, flown by Major Wayne Myers, was forced to crash land on an old French airstrip in the middle of Communist positions at one end of the valley. As he clambered out of the cockpit, expecting to be captured, he had to take cover to avoid the heavy gunfire being directed at him by Communist troops. As he ran around the carcass of his plane and dove to the tarmac, he saw another A-1E Skyraider landing and then flashing by him on the runway. He recognized his wingman, Major Bernard Fisher, and ran after him down the debris-littered runway amid a hail of bullets. After several hundred meters, he caught up to Fisher as he turned and taxied back toward him. Myers jumped up on the wing, then dove head-first into the open cockpit behind Fisher's single pilot's seat, his feet still sticking out in the breeze as they took off. Major Fisher became the first Air Force recipient of the Medal of Honor in Vietnam for this daring feat.

In late October 1966, the North Vietnamese 101st Regiment and the Viet Cong 9th Division attacked the US Special Forces camp at Suoi Da, then lay in ambush waiting for the American forces they knew would rush to the rescue. Eventually, elements of the US 1st, 4th and 25th Infantry Divisions

entered the battle. Although the Communists had laid their
trap well, they had not considered the massive air power
available to US troops: within 9 days, they were crushed.
More than 2500 tactical sorties were flown in support of
American forces, including 225 by B-52s. By the first week
in November, the Communists had had enough, and one night
they disappeared, leaving the bodies of 1100 of their soldiers
behind.

This operation was one of the first big ones, and air power
served wide and varied purposes. In addition to their impact
as a weapon of force, aircraft also flew 3300 tactical airlift
sorties, bringing 8900 tons of supplies to the front and moving
more than 11,000 men to and from the battlefield.

Tactical air support was used increasingly in the III Corps
area through 1966 and 1967. US forces engaged in Operations
Birmingham and Attleboro in War Zone C, as well as in
Operation Cedar Falls in the Iron Triangle, enjoyed powerful
air support that generally broke whatever resistance the Communists attempted. Operation Junction City in War Zone C
(chapter 3) provided several occasions when Communist
forces gambled big and tried to overwhelm US bases in spite
of withering artillery and air support. Although they lost many
soldiers in these attempts, none of them were successful.

In the wake of these American successes in rooting out
and destroying main Communist forces, the potential impact
of B-52 strikes was just beginning to be realized by American
commanders. In November 1967, at the battle of Dak To in
the Central Highlands, American forces were being savaged
by waves of North Vietnamese regulars. This was the first
real emergency where B-52s were called on to rescue hard-
pressed American forces, but their devastating bomb loads
—they could carry up to 84 750-lb bombs, or over 30 tons
of explosives—completely turned the tables on the Communists and drove them from the battlefield, leaving 1600
dead. From that time on, whenever ground commanders were
hard pressed, their most fervent prayer was for a B-52 strike
to churn the earth where the enemy was concealed. When
such strikes were available, they invariably saved the day.

Throughout 1967, major American and South Vietnamese

operations nationwide were the beneficiaries of tens of thousands of tactical air sorties; these in turn were responsible for countless Communist deaths. Air support quickly became a routine part of the war, available to smash an obdurate enemy position, prepare a trail for friendly movement, insert or extract troops from hot spots and shake the mountains nightly in groping efforts to harass and interdict Communist troop movement. In January 1968, the North Vietnamese began their seige of Khe Sanh, where combined tactical and logistical air support got its hardest test to date, and eventually carried the day for the Americans. On 31 January the Tet Offensive erupted across the nation, and air support was key to many of the specific battles fought over individual towns and cities, particularly that for Hue.

After the major Communist onslaught was thrown back, a long pause ensued. The war in South Vietnam had been largely won by South Vietnamese forces and their American allies, and Communist forces divided up into small units and sought refuge in mountain fastnesses or inside neighboring Cambodia or Laos. American air power was not called on again massively until the South Vietnamese-American incursion into Cambodia in April 1970. Another long pause ensued, followed by Lam Son 719, the South Vietnamese lunge into Laos in January 1971. American air support was the crucial element there that saved face for the South Vietnamese and prevented a shameful rout. Then, just before Easter 1972, the North Vietnamese ventured everything on a massive, tank-studded invasion of South Vietnam on three fronts. Once again, American air support in South Vietnam was decisive, in combination with massive renewed bombing of North Vietnam. In August 1973, American forces were forbidden by law to carry on military operations in or over Indochina, and that was the end of American air support in South Vietnam. But while support of US and South Vietnamese forces in South Vietnam was the focus of American air efforts, US Air Force and Navy planes were also carrying on major bombing campaigns in other parts of Indochina, particularly in North Vietnam.

After the retaliatory raids of early 1965, American bombing

missions against North Vietnam were formally structured as Operation Rolling Thunder. This campaign was carried out to show the North Vietnamese the seriousness of American support for the South Vietnamese Government, and through gradual escalation of damage inflicted on their homeland, to punish them until they stopped their aggression in South Vietnam. But American leaders failed to perceive the true North Vietnamese situation. Theirs was a society based largely on subsistence agriculture, whose light and rudimentary industry was not crucial to their existence. They received all the military weapons and supplies they needed (including MiG fighters and Surface-to-Air Missiles) from their Soviet and Chinese allies, and their only production requirement was for young soldiers to fill their ranks in South Vietnam. The American bombing campaign helped foster a siege mentality of resistance against wicked outsiders in the North Vietnamese people. And as Rolling Thunder progressed, it became increasingly clear that Ho Chi Minh and his lieutenants were dedicated Leninist-Stalinists who would never be swayed from their political goals by hardships inflicted on their people.

As the targets available to American bombers increased and moved north into the heartland, many pauses were made to negotiate, with the hope that North Vietnam would stop or reduce its aggression in South Vietnam. But these pauses produced only words, and the North Vietnamese used the respites to move their light industry underground and disperse their population across open farmland in preparation for the next wave of bombing. Rolling Thunder was carried out in four general phases by US Air Force planes flying out of Thailand and US Navy planes flying from aircraft carriers at Yankee Station in the Tonkin Gulf.

The first phase began in the summer of 1965 and involved systematic attacks on North Vietnam's military transportation system. Bombing raids were concentrated on infiltration routes in the southern part of North Vietnam, with attacks creeping steadily north over time and striking an expanding array of targets. The second phase lasted only through the month of July 1966, during which time some 80 percent of

North Vietnam's oil storage capacity was destroyed. This had some immediate short-term effect on the population, but the oil supplies were soon replaced by imports from Communist allies, and the destruction had no discernible effect whatever on North Vietnamese forces in South Vietnam.

The third phase occurred in the spring of 1967, when a whole host of previously forbidden targets were opened to bombing raids. Urban power plants, raw material factories, ammunition dumps, cement plants and airfields were all pounded by American aircraft, but the North Vietnamese remained impervious to such damage as the war in the south smoldered, then burst into flame in the 1968 Tet Offensive. The fourth and final phase came when President Johnson announced a partial halt to the bombing of North Vietnam that would begin on 1 April 1968. On 1 November 1968, Operation Rolling Thunder ended.

On 7 August 1964, Lt Everett Alvarez was flying an A-4 Skyhawk off the USS *Constellation* in one of the first retaliatory raids on North Vietnam when he was shot down by ground fire and became the first American prisoner of war. For reasons that are still not entirely clear, he and hundreds of other American POWs were systematically tortured by their North Vietnamese captors for a number of years. Finally, in March 1973, Lt Alvarez and 590 other American POWs were released as a function of the Paris Agreements that had been signed by the United States, South Vietnam, North Vietnam and the Viet Cong. Over 2500 missing American fliers remained unaccounted for, even though many of them had been assumed captured after they were shot down. But the North Vietnamese said they had no information on any other Americans, and repeated efforts to gain more information have been unsuccessful.

As Rolling Thunder began regular operations, North Vietnamese MiG fighters were occasionally seen hovering nearby, but they avoided contact. Finally, on 4 April 1965, two US Air Force F-105s were shot down by slower, more maneuverable MiG-17s. Over the following two months, more air-to-air combat took place between American and North Vietnamese fighters, but no planes went down as a result. Then, on 17 June, two MiG-17s were shot down by US Navy F-4 Phantoms, and a third was dropped by a propeller-driven US Navy A-1E Skyraider. Just as the MiG-17s had used their greater turning ability to bag two F-105s back in April, so the slower-still Skyraider had used the same trick to nail a MiG.

By August 1965, the North Vietnamese began installing Surface-to-Air Missiles (SAMs) as integral parts of their air-defense system, and they began bringing down American aircraft. The Navy and the Air Force each instituted their own policies to deal with SAMs, including flying at low levels until they arrived in the target area or firing missiles at the SAM sites that would home in on their target acquisition radar. But the principal, and most effective, defense was the use of special electronic-counter-measure aircraft packed with high-tech gear with which to interdict or fool entire sections of the North Vietnamese air-defense system.

During Rolling Thunder's existence, 922 American aircraft were lost to hostile action over North Vietnam, while 500,000 tons of bombs were dropped on that country. But the desired effect of the operation—forcing the North Vietnamese to stop their aggression in South Vietnam—was never realized, and it was the United States that finally backed down.

A major portion of the air war in Indochina involved American efforts to stem the flow of North Vietnamese supplies and reinforcements into South Vietnam. Initially, three main channels were used for this: the Ho Chi Minh Trail, a network of interwoven roads and trails down the Laotian Panhandle next to the South Vietnamese border; cargo ships to Sihanoukville, the Cambodian port, and thence across Cambodia into III and IV Corps regions of South Vietnam; and smaller vessels to deliver resupplies to Communist agents waiting at points along the entire South Vietnamese coast. But the US Navy began to restrict the latter channel with Operation Market Time in the middle 1960s, and Prince Sihanouk's fall from power in 1970 brought an end to Communist use of Cambodia's port facilities. Both events resulted in increased dependence by the North Vietnamese on the Ho Chi Minh Trail, which made it an even more attractive target for US aircraft.

In 1965 a methodical air operation to interdict traffic on the Ho Chi Minh Trail, Operation Steel Tiger, was launched by US Air Force and Navy aircraft. By their nature, missions flown here differed from those flown over North and South Vietnam. Dropping bombs into largely uninhabited expanses of jungle meant that little effort was required to avoid collateral damage to civilians. The close co-ordination with ground forces required for effective support of friendly troops in combat was not a concern, nor was there the tense alertness required over North Vietnam to avoid SAMs and other air-defense weapons. The mission was simply to stop the flow of troops and supplies.

That sounds much easier than it was, of course. The Ho Chi Minh Trail was a profusion of parallel and crisscrossing roads and trails. The terrain was heavily jungled, often with a triple canopy that concealed movement to observers in the sky, and after the American bombing campaign started, the North Vietnamese ran most of their convoys at night, making them truly invisible to the naked eye. The Americans had two basic choices: they could try to hit the convoys as they moved, or they could try to interdict the trail itself. Both approaches were used.

By far the largest amount of ordnance was delivered in efforts to destroy the array of roads that made up the Trail. Early bombing runs were made by US Air Force B-57s out of South Vietnam, but these were soon replaced by Air Force, Navy and Marine fighter-bombers with more sophisticated delivery systems. The North Vietnamese had tens of thousands of support troops stationed in the Laotian Panhandle whose sole responsibility was maintenance of the Trail, and bomb craters could often be filled and free passage restored in a matter of hours. Consequently, American fliers tried to concentrate their ordnance on 'choke points' where traffic was necessarily congested—bridges, mountain passes, narrow valleys. B-52s began to overfly the Trail with great regularity, and their bomb loads could literally change the topography of a given area. But always the North Vietnamese workers were quickly on the spot with shovels and simple earthmoving equipment. Defoliants were heavily sprayed in some areas to expose the trail to view from the air, but these efforts had only mixed results.

The actual truck-killing was best performed by C-47, C-119 and C-130 gunships. These were large cargo aircraft, specially configured to mount Gatling guns that could fire 6000 rounds of 20mm ammunition per minute, of which they carried literally tons. These aircraft were equipped with sophisticated night-vision and electronic targeting equipment that, when adequately supported by sensors on the ground below, allowed them to see and target North Vietnamese truck convoys moving under jungle canopies on the blackest nights. They were able to loiter at low speeds high above the target area, waiting for convoys to arrive, then pounce on them like a duck on a row of June bugs. On some nights, the Ho Chi Minh Trail was literally a giant shooting gallery.

The US Government made a major effort to halt or reduce traffic on the Trail through the heavy use of air power, but their success in this endeavor is difficult to measure. The only person, finally, who really knew how much of a given supply convoy ever reached Communist forces in South Vietnam was the North Vietnamese Quartermaster Officer who accompanied it on its entire trip. Whether US air attacks destroyed a significant proportion of the supplies and reinforcements destined for South Vietnam or only slowed their transit is something of a moot point. It is self-evident that enough got through to keep the Communist forces going, for the North Vietnamese never made a single political concession to the Americans to reduce the air attacks against the Ho Chi Minh Trail.

A different war entirely was being waged in Northern Laos between the Communist Pathet Lao and the Royal Laotian Government (RLG). In support of Prime Minister Souvanna Phouma's government, the United States had established Operation Barrel Roll in 1964, a campaign of tactical air strikes against Pathet Lao forces supported by the North Vietnamese. This operation lasted until the spring of 1973. American aircraft were also crucial to the survival against vastly superior forces of the private army of General Vang Pao. The army consisted of some 5000 Meo hill tribesmen indigenous to

Laos who had been trained by the CIA. They fought an irregular war against the Communists, and were a key factor in defending an area of the country that included Vientiane, the national capital.

The war in northern Laos swung back and forth until 1970, when Pathet Lao troops began to control the important Plain of Jars. The first B-52 strikes went into northern Laos in February 1970, and thousands more B-52 sorties followed it over the next few years. Peace talks between the RLG and the Pathet Lao were started in 1972, and in April 1973 the last major American air strike in northern Laos was made by B-52s south of the Plain of Jars. That summer, the United States ended all air operations over a country destined to fall under control of the North Vietnamese Communists.

The air war arrived in Cambodia much later than in the rest of Indochina. Prince Sihanouk, the Cambodian ruler, had long claimed a neutral position in the Vietnam War, although he allowed use of his country's major port by the North Vietnamese for passage of enormous shipments of supplies destined for Communist forces in South Vietnam. He also acquiesced in North Vietnamese construction of vast storage and support facilities just inside Cambodia along the South Vietnamese border, from which the Communists managed and supported their war against the South Vietnamese Government. But the North Vietnamese soon wore out their welcome, and in 1968 and 1969, Sihanouk privately informed US leaders that he would not object to secret bombing of Communist positions inside Cambodia.

Starting in March 1969, newly elected President Nixon launched such a secret bombing campaign. Over the next 14 months, B-52s flew 4300 sorties and dropped 120,000 tons of bombs on suspected Communist positions inside Cambodia. In March 1970, Sihanouk was overthrown and replaced by a stridently anti-Communist Lon Nol, who ordered Communist troops out of his country. The Americans and South Vietnamese were asked to enter Cambodia and clean out the Communist sanctuaries, and on 29 April, they did just that. Air support in this two-month series of operations was a key element in their success, but when American and South Vietnamese forces withdrew at the end of June, Communist troops began to take over great chunks of Cambodian territory. By the end of 1970, they controlled roughly half the country, and Lon Nol's troops were hard pressed by North Vietnamese forces. American air power was of crucial important in assuring the survival of the government, causing Prince Sihanouk to comment from exile in Peking that Lon Nol clung to power 'only through the intervention of the US Air Force.'

While US ground forces were not to return to to assist the fight against Communism, the South Vietnamese did on a number of occasions, always with US air support. Finally, in August 1973, all American forces were with drawn from Indochina, and Cambodia, too was abandoned to the relentless Communist onslaught.

After the end of Operation Rolling Thunder in 1968, bombing attacks into North Vietnam became infrequent, and the systematic missions had ended. When the North Vietnamese launched their Easter Offensive invasion of South Vietnam in 1972, part of the American reaction included mining North Vietnamese harbors and sending major bombing raids, including waves of B-52s, against virtually all of the North. This operation, code-named Linebacker, had far more freedom in target selection than had been the case with Rolling Thunder. The raids lasted until 22 October, by which time 10 MiG bases, 6 major power plants and all large oil-storage facilities in North Vietnam had been destroyed. American planes now had 'smart' bombs, guided to their targets by lasers or TV cameras, and succeeded in bringing down key bridges that had survived numerous attacks during Rolling Thunder.

The final tally for Linebacker showed 41,000 sorties by B-52s and other Air Force and Navy fighter-bombers, and 156,000 tons of bombs dropped on North Vietnam. The cost was 75 aircraft lost, but Linebacker appeared to temporarily cripple North Vietnam and its connections to China by railway.

In December 1972, peace discussions had reached an impasse, as the North Vietnamese decided simply to wait for unilateral American withdrawal from Indochina. Angered by this intransigence, President Nixon ordered a massive bombing attack against North Vietnam, including targets in the Hanoi-Haiphong area. The raids lasted for 11 days, during which 700 sorties were made by B-52s and 1000 by fighter-bombers, delivering 20,000 tons of bombs across all of North Vietnam. American losses were 26 planes, including 15 B-52s. Of the 30-odd MiGs North Vietnam had left, eight were shot down during this period, including two by B-52 tail gunners. Over the first week, the North Vietnamese fired over 1000 SAMs, but their air defenses were pounded into rubble: during the last two days of the operation, American planes flew over North Vietnam with impunity.

The air war over Indochina created the opportunity for American forces to use highly sophisticated and destructive airborne weapons systems that were rightfully feared by their Communist adversaries. Their availability on the battlefield often won the day for South Vietnamese and American ground forces, even those who had been outgunned, outwitted or outmaneuvered by the North Vietnamese. But the rapid, cost-free availability to South Vietnamese and American forces of powerful 'Death From Above' aircraft gave rise to an unfortunate and unthinking dependence on them. Because it was easier, this reliance replaced much of the hard work that would have been involved in building a South Vietnamese military able to withstand Communist pressure. But whether that was ever a realistic possibility awaits the judgment of history.

THE NAVAL WAR

The major escalation of US participation in the Vietnam War was precipitated by North Vietnamese attacks on two US destroyers, the *Maddox* and the *Turner Joy*, as they steamed through international waters in August 1964. At the time, covert operations against North Vietnam were taking place through at least two independent programs from the sea. The first was Operations Plan (OPLAN) 34, involving raids on North Vietnamese coastal installations by South Vietnamese Navy and Marine forces. While Americans provided advice and logistical support, South Vietnamese vessels and military forces carried out the actual attacks. The second program, DE SOTO, involved the use of American vessels to observe the activity of the North Vietnamese Navy and to measure the capabilities of North Vietnamese radar and other electronic surveillance equipment.

The *Maddox* was conducting a DE SOTO patrol on 2 August 1964, when it was attacked by three North Vietnamese torpedo boats. At the time, the *Maddox* was 28 miles from the North Vietnamese coast, clearly in international waters. It happened that, unknown to the *Maddox* Commander, an OPLAN 34 raid had taken place on the night of 31 July against a group of North Vietnamese islands some 130 miles away from the location of the *Maddox* when she was attacked. Whether the North Vietnamese had assumed the *Maddox* had played a role in this raid is unknown, but on 3 August she was ordered farther north, away from the scene of the South Vietnamese operations, and was joined by the *Turner Joy*. The President ordered air cover for their operation, and directed that, if attacked again in international waters, they respond by destroying the attacking vessels.

Thereafter, the two ships went no closer than 16 miles from the North Vietnamese coast, remaining continuously in international waters. On the night of 4 August 1964, the *Maddox* reported that both ships were again under attack by North Vietnamese vessels. Because of terrible weather conditions, the details of the engagement were never clear, but as Secretary of Defense McNamara later testified to Congress, the fact that the North Vietnamese actually attacked the two American ships was never in doubt.

Before dawn on 5 August, American air strikes against North Vietnamese torpedo-boat bases took place, a response specifically authorized by the President of the United States. On 7 August 1964, both Houses of the US Congress overwhelmingly passed the Tonkin Gulf Resolution, approving such military action. It resolved 'that the Congress approve and support the determination of the President, as Commander in Chief, to take all necessary measures to repel any armed attack against the forces of the United States and to prevent further aggression.' The resolution also stated that the United States is 'prepared, as the President determines, to take all necessary steps, including the use of armed force, to assist any Member or Protocol State of the Southeast Asia Collective Defense Treaty requesting assistance in defense of its freedom.' So began America's major involvement in the fight against Communism that was to rage through Indochina for over a decade. Some key American leaders thought at first that a few devastating air raids against major North Vietnamese military targets would bring them to their senses. But this was not to be, and within less than a year, major US troop units were deployed to South Vietnam.

The role of the US Navy in the Vietnam War was largely logistical: the only efficient way to transport the enormous stores of equipment and supplies needed, and at first even the troops themselves, was by ship. But the Navy also played key roles in the conduct of the war itself. The major part played by aircraft launched from aircraft carriers located at Dixie Station and Yankee station has already been discussed. US Navy operations also attempted to seal off the coast of South Vietnam and patrolled the navigable rivers with their smaller craft. Additionally, there were joint US Navy-Army operations in the Mekong Delta known as the 'Riverine' war.

Soon after the Tonkin Gulf incidents, the US Government decided to support the South Vietnamese, as they had often been requested to do, in their efforts to prevent Communist shipping of supplies into South Vietnam by sea. This involved lengthy operations, code-named 'Market Time,' by shallow-draft Navy vessels that would patrol the coast and, when required, stop, search and seize many types of vessels. These patrols were initially made by US Coast Guard cutters, supplemented by 50-foot aluminum-hulled 'Swift' boats. In addition to the patrol boats, however, Navy aircraft also played a major role in Market Time. As a complement to the patrol boats, a number of Navy air patrol squadrons participated in surveillance operations along the South Vietnamese coast. The aircraft used were the P-2 Neptunes, the P-3 Orions and the P-5 Marlins. These were relatively slow, lumbering aircraft that operated on long, boring patrols along the entire length of the South Vietnamese coast. But the electronic sensors they carried quickly picked up suspicious craft and relayed the information to *Swift*-type boats waiting below.

For the aircraft, actually, Operation Market Time included three different missions: Market Time, Yankee Station and OSAP (ocean surveillance patrols). Over half the missions flown were devoted to sealing the coast, by relaying radar indications of suspicious vessels to waiting patrol boats, as described above. The most important targets sought were the large, steel-hulled trawlers supplied to North Vietnam by the People's Republic of China, because of the large volume of supplies they could carry. But because of their very size and the clear 'signature' they gave to radar, Market Time was quite effective in disrupting their traffic, causing the Communists to break their shipments down into loads that could be carried by smaller wooden-hulled vessels. The Market Time patrol boats disrupted much of this traffic as well, but because of the time required for searching a given vessel and the huge volume of small craft plying the coastal waters of South Vietnam, it is clear that many of the Communist supply runs got through.

The Yankee Station missions were flown at night and at low altitudes—often below 500 feet. The aircraft were looking for North Vietnamese aircraft or torpedo boats preparing to make a run against the major US Navy fleet on station in the area, or for downed US air crews. The OSAP missions generally involved shadowing Russian or Chinese ships suspected of being involved in the Communist resupply effort, but were frequently fruitless.

Market Time aircraft missions were generally of 10 to 12 hours duration, and although they were not the flashy stuff of the evening news, they contributed significantly to the war effort. The operation of their partner Swift boats, however, more often involved the very real danger of gunfire and death. The joint air-sea operations carried out by these forces were quite disruptive of the North Vietnamese support efforts and resulted in ever-greater dependence by the Communists on their more reliable overland resupply routes down the Ho Chi Minh Trail.

Throughout the Vietnam War, the key area of the country of South Vietnam was the Mekong River Delta. Extending south and west from Saigon, the Delta covers some 40,000 square kilometers and was home to over eight million people—some 60 percent of the population of the entire country living on 20 percent of its land area. An extremely fertile alluvial plain, the Delta was formed over millennia as silt carried by the Mekong River and the numerous tributaries through which it meanders to the sea slowly built up. Most of the Delta is covered by seasonally flooded rice paddies, and only one hard-surface road—Route 4—connects Saigon with the farthest reaches of the Ca Mau Peninsula. Most of the other roads linking districts and even provinces are dirt and were often unusable, because of either the war or the weather.

The result was that the use of conventional wheeled or tracked vehicles was not reliable, particularly during the wet half of the year. During the six-month dry season, the rice paddies were hard dirt and would support wheeled or light tracked vehicles, but cross-country movement was still severly restricted by myriad canals, streams, dikes, rivers and ditches. During the six-month wet season, even movement by road was limited and unpredictable, but a highly developed inland waterway system resulted in almost ideal conditions for transportation of troops and control of all water-borne movement by the use of armed and armored boats. There are around 2400 kilometers of navigable natural waterways in the Delta, supplemented by another 4000 kilometers of man-made canals. During the wet season, most of these canals were navigable, and shallow-draft boats could often simply traverse wide expanses of open territory seasonally flooded to a depth of up to several meters.

The Mekong Delta was in constant political ferment, and during the middle 1960s, control of the population was slipping from the South Vietnamese Government to the North Vietnamese-supported Communist rebels, the Viet Cong. In 1966 there were some 40,000 ARVN troops in the Delta, divided into three infantry divisions, five Ranger Battalions, and three armored cavalry squadrons. But there were also some 80,000 Viet Cong there at the same time, divided into three regiments, 30 battalions, and 60 separate companies. Of these, only 20,000 were full-time soldiers, while 10,000 were political cadre and 50,000 were part-time irregular guerrillas. US forces in the Delta were limited to Navy forces on Market-Time operations and an Aviation Battalion.

The US Navy launched Operation Game Warden in 1966 in an effort to control the waterways and so restrict Viet Cong movement. Some 120 river patrol boats (PBR) were used for this operation, working out of numerous river's-edge base camps in the northern sections of the Delta. Fast, highly maneuverable craft using water-jet propulsion, the PBRs were armed with 50-caliber machine guns and belt-fed 40mm grenade launchers. They packed a powerful punch to be used as a glancing blow, but they were not heavily armored and could do little more than interdict the use of the waterways by the Viet Cong, and even this on a chancy basis.

But the Viet Cong had long maintained a number of major base areas they considered safe, within which their dominion was not challenged. Some of these areas were the Rung Sat Special Zone, the Cocoanut Grove in Go Cong Province, the Cam Son Secret Zone west of My Tho, the U Minh forest on the western coast and the Seven Mountains region on the Cambodian border. Together, these areas formed islands across the entire Delta, among which major Viet Cong or North Vietnamese units could easily slip during the night, and which could be used as staging areas for major attacks without warning. It was clear that in order to defeat Communist forces in the Delta, American and South Vietnamese troops had to challenge and defeat them here, on what both sides considered their safe base areas.

In 1966 the South Vietnamese Government agreed to allow an American division to be stationed in the Delta, but there were logistical problems involved. The Delta was heavily populated, and there was little permanently dry land that was not already inhabited either by civilians or by South Vietnamese military forces. This was partially resolved when one of the three Brigades in the assigned US division was stationed on Navy LSTs converted into barrack ships. These ships could be moved around the Delta with considerable freedom to confront changing Communist threats, and a flotilla of supporting smaller LCM-6 boats was used by the troops in the conduct of operations. With variations in their armament and layout, these LCMs could be used as Armored Troop Carriers (ATC), 'Monitor' gunboats, command and communication boats, refuelers or minesweepers. This new combined-arms team, properly titled the Mobile Afloat Force, quickly became known as the Riverine Force. The Viet Cong never tried to challenge for control of the waterways with their own armored craft, but rather relied exclusively on the use of carefully prepared ambushes from the banks of the waterways. But the Riverine Force brought more than floating firepower, for once a Communist troop concentration was located, infantry forces could be landed nearby and, using supporting fire from the boats as well as artillery and tactical air strikes, close with and destroy the enemy.

The Riverine Force consisted of the 2nd Brigade of the US 9th Infantry Division and the ships and boats of the US Navy Task Force 117. They began to operate together in the spring of 1967, and in June moved through the Rung Sat Special Zone and Can Giuoc District of Long An Province. Both were long-time safe base areas for the Viet Cong, but the Riverine Force left only death and destruction in its wake. The Communists soon learned that they had little chance against the combined water-air-land elements they now faced, and began to revert to their favorite tactic in the face of superior force: they simply disappeared.

As the elements of the Riverine Force fought, they also learned, and their operation soon ran smoothly, even against determined opposition. A typical engagement will illustrate the realities of the war fought by the US Army and Navy in the Mekong Delta.

At 3:00 AM the half-awake US Army troops of the Riverine Force clambered down from the USS *Colleton* barracks ship into their smaller ATCs, then quickly fell back asleep as their flotilla began to move up the Mekong River. It was 15 September, 1967. The Riverine Force was moving to attack two Viet Cong Battalions, the 514th and the 263rd, believed to be located at a bend in the Rach Ba Rai River north of its intersection with the Mekong, in the heart of the Cam Son Secret Zone.

Two battalions, the 3rd of the 60th Infantry and the 3rd of the 47th Infantry, were to move up the Rach Ba Rai in assault boats before first light. The 3rd of the 60th was to bypass the suspected enemy positions and land to their north at beaches White One and Two, while the 3rd of the 47th was to disembark south of the Communist locations at beaches Red One and Two. The armored flotilla was then to interdict the Rach Ba Rai between the two infantry battalions, while the 5th Battalion 60th Infantry moved overland from the east in M-113 armored personnel carriers and closed the circle. Once this had occurred, the plan said that the three artillery batteries attached to the Riverine Force would pound the surrounded

Viet Cong battalions, and tactical air strikes would finish them off.

There were administrative delays, but by 7:00 AM the armored flotilla began to move up the Rach Ba Rai. Dawn had arrived at 6:00 AM, but the narrow waterway was still covered with early-morning fog as the boats moved along at ten miles per hour. The convoy carrying the 3rd of the 60th was led by two empty ATCs acting as minesweepers, and by 7:30 they had passed the Red beaches and were rounding the bend where the Viet Cong battalions were thought to be. Suddenly the calm was shattered by the explosions of two RPG2 anti-tank rockets against the starboard hull of one of the mine-sweepers. Shouts rang out that they had hit a mine, but within seconds, this was contradicted by a hail of automatic-weapons fire from both banks.

Soon, more and more boats were hit by RPGs as it became apparent that the entire flotilla had been caught in the killing zone of an ambush. The second minesweeper was hit by four RPG2s, and began to drift out of control toward the eastern bank. American crews opened up with everything they had, and gunsmoke soon formed an impenetrable fog with the morning mist as both sides fired point-blank into each other's faces. In short order, even the infantry troops being transported were firing their rifles at the river banks, adding to the hail of death pouring out of the American boats from 20mm and 40mm guns, 81mm direct fire mortars, M-60 machine guns and heavy 50-caliber machine guns. But despite their volume of fire, anti-tank rockets, recoilless-rifle rounds and heavy machine-gun fire kept pounding into their hulls. The Communist positions were in mud bunkers with overhead cover, some of them right at the water line, and it was impossible to see anything except muzzle flashes. Confusion began to take its toll now, as some boats seemed to drift helplessly, while others churned past them in a desperate attempt to get out of the killing zone. The Battalion Commander of the 3rd of the 60th was overhead in a helicopter, helplessly monitoring the radio traffic from the battle raging below him. Meanwhile, artillery forward observers were orbiting in spotter aircraft and calling fire from the three Riverine Force artillery batteries on the Communist positions. But the ambush site was some 1500 meters long, and the Communist bunkers were largely hidden from aircraft by fog and smoke. The only way it seemed they could be knocked out was by a direct hit, which would depend as much on luck as on anything else.

Within ten minutes after the ambush was sprung, the forward movement of the flotilla had stopped, although individual boats continued to dart back and forth. Then, as the Battalion Commander watched from above, one ATC broke out of the killing zone and churned north toward beach White Two. Enthused, the Battalion Commander sent the word down to his troops to follow the charge, but this order was countermanded by the Naval commander of the flotilla. In order for the flotilla to continue north, it had to be preceded by a minesweeper, and the Naval officer in command decided that both minesweepers were too disabled to perform this task. At 7:50—some twenty minutes after the ambush had been sprung—he ordered the flotilla to withdraw and reassemble in the vicinity of the Red Beaches to the south. Although all the boats in the flotilla had been heavily hit, none had been sunk or lost their engines, and all were able to comply with this order, some more quickly than others. Four Air Force A-37s arrived at 8:00 AM with napalm and high-explosive bombs, and these helped the last boats slip out of the killing zone.

Meanwhile, the single boat to land at White Two contained the Commander of B Company and one of his platoons. As they left the boat, they were immediately engaged by strong Communist forces, and the fact that they were the only boat to reach the landing made them even more inviting targets. With the help of intense artillery bombardment, however, they were able to break contact and re-embark. The pilot had the boat going full speed when it re-entered the ambush area, and miraculously, it was hit by only one RPG2 rocket as it sped back toward safety. Although this rocket killed one man and wounded four more, the surviving men on the boat felt deeply grateful for their lives when they rejoined the flotilla at the Red Beach area.

The dead and wounded were transferred to medical boats there, and reinforcements for the Navy crews brought them back up to full strength. Artillery fire and air strikes were lighting up both sides of the stream while this was going on, for it was becoming increasingly clear that landing at the White Beaches was the critical part of this operation, and the gauntlet would have to be run once again.

By 10:00 AM, the American forces were ready for another try, but this time there would be no surprise on either side. As the boats entered the ambush site, every gun was firing. But their fire was returned by the Viet Cong with renewed vigor and ferocity. One of the lead minesweepers was hit again by two RPG2 rockets: then all the boats began to take hits. In one boat, eighteen men from one platoon were hit and four were killed. Only five men from that platoon would disembark at White Two, while the rest stayed on board for the ride back to the medical boats. But this time, everyone knew what they faced, and the boat crews got their craft through the killing zone as fast as possible.

As the boats arrived at White Two, they began to disgorge troops. But the Viet Cong had been put on notice by the single boat that had made it through the ambush earlier, and the beach at White Two was another killing zone. Three companies landed there, but they were stuck for hours in the thick strip of jungle along the river. Heavy air strikes helped them to reduce the pressure from Communist gunfire, and just after noon they were able to break out into open fields some 200 meters east of the river. But this was little more than a shooting galley, with intense small-arms fire being directed at them from positions east, south and even north of them. Progress south through the afternoon was slow.

Meanwhile, the 3rd of the 47th had landed at the Red beaches with little immediate opposition, but once ashore, heavy Communist fire was directed on them from well-prepared positions. Movement was slow and cautious, as the American troops moved forward against fiercely defended Communist positions. To the east, the drive of the 5th Battalion 60th Infantry had been stalled, and they had been reinforced by the 2nd Battalion 60th Infantry, brought to their support by helicopter.

The plans for trapping the two Viet Cong battalions on their home ground were fading fast, disappearing with the afternoon light. By 5:00 PM, all American units were heavily engaged with Viet Cong forces, and the goals of each battalion had been readjusted. Gone was any hope of cutting off enemy escape routes, replaced with concern that each of the American battalions be able to form secure night defensive positions in strange territory that had long been a Viet Cong base area.

The night passed uneventfully, and in the morning it was clear why: Viet Cong forces had completely withdrawn from the area, leaving behind 79 bodies. American casualties had been 17 killed and 123 wounded. This had been a typical Riverine Force operation. Limited in scope and scale, this was the way the war was fought in the Mekong River Delta. The Riverine Force continued its operations until August of 1969, at which time its boats were turned over to the Vietnamese Navy or to a new US Navy Operation, 'Sea Lords,' whose two goals were to stop the flow of Communist supplies entering the Mekong River Delta, particularly across the inundated Plain of Reeds on the Cambodian border, and to exert control of vital trans-delta inland waterways.

By late 1968, most of the Delta had been cleared of major Communist forces. Route 4, which had been closed to traffic by the Viet Cong from 1964 through 1967, was reopened, and the bountiful farm produce from the Delta began to flow smoothly to the marketplace again. US Navy operations along the Cambodian border in late 1969 were also successful, and the fact that by then most of the fertile farm land of the Delta was firmly under control of the South Vietnamese Government was evidence of the contributions they had made while fighting the war afloat.

THE EXPLOSION

Tet 1968

In the three years after major American combat units began to arrive in South Vietnam in March of 1965, the whole nature of the war in that country changed. North Vietnamese Communist forces in South Vietnam, along with their indigenous Viet Cong allies, had first decided to challenge the American troops. They launched a number of human-wave attacks by vastly superior forces against American positions—General Giap's favorite tactic, which had overwhelmed the French at Dien Bien Phu. The battles in the Ia Drang Valley and during Operation Junction City are perhaps the best examples of this strategy. But times had changed, and superior American air and artillery power had blunted subsequent Communist onslaughts and thrown them back with great loss of life to the attackers.

This had caused some rethinking of tactics in Communist ranks. It was clear that Communist troops would be soundly thrashed by American forces on the conventional battlefield because of vastly superior weaponry. But the psychological impact on France and the rest of the world caused by the victory over the French at Dien Bien Phu had been remarkable. It seemed, in the fall of 1967, that history might be repeating itself: American Marines were prepared to defend an isolated outpost at Khe Sanh with the same resolve shown by the French at Dien Bien Phu years earlier.

It is probable that General Giap made the decision to besiege Khe Sanh in late January 1968. It is also probable that, hailed as a military genius at home and abroad, he made the decision to launch the massive, co-ordinated surprise attacks against South Vietnamese and American bases during the Tet 1968 cease-fire.

It is clear from the record, however, that Giap is far from a military genius. When he took over control of the Viet Minh rebels fighting the French in the late 1940s, his background was as a political idealogue—he had received only one year of rudimentary military training in China. His tactics were those he had learned from the Chinese Communists: massed human-wave attacks with vastly superior forces would ensure victory, and the successful commander must be oblivious to his own losses or those inflicted on civilians, keeping the victory on the battlefield as his only goal.

Giap's lack of flexibility and other short-comings as both commander and strategist were apparent again at Khe Sanh and in the suicidal attacks he launched during the 1968 Tet Offensive. But while the latter may have been a major military blunder, its impact on the United States and the rest of the world was far more dramatic even than Dien Bien Phu's: it marked the beginning of the end of US military presence in South Vietnam. The evidence indicates that the political outcome was a result of either some phenomenally lucky fumbling by the national leadership of North Vietnam, or the shrewdest, most insightful planning seen on the world stage for some time—or perhaps a little of both. At any rate, the actual insight of North Vietnamese leaders into possible outcomes is unimportant for a review of the actual events.

The most important holiday for the Vietnamese people is the Tet Lunar New Year. It lasts for seven days, and is a time for family reunions and celebration. Each year since 1965, 24-hour truces had been observed by the Communists, the South Vietnamese and the Americans for the Western Christmas Day and New Year's holidays, and for slightly longer periods for the Vietnamese Tet. The Vietnamese economy generally pauses for a week during Tet while the entire population participates in feasts, celebrations, and noisy public demonstrations.

In 1968 the Viet Cong announced a seven-day Tet truce to last from 27 January until 3 February. The South Vietnamese Government and the US forces, for their part, announced a 36-hour cease-fire, to be effective from the evening of 29 January until morning of 31 January. The Americans made an exception for the I Corps Region bordering on the DMZ in northern South Vietnam, where intelligence showed ominous movements by North Vietnamese troops that threatened US positions. The Americans had hard evidence of a major North Vietnamese and Viet Cong offensive in the near future, but there was no information on timing. There were some reports of an attack planned to coincide with the Tet holiday, but many such reports had been heard in the past and proved to be without substance; they received little credence.

In fact, Communist forces in South Vietnam, primarily the Viet Cong, were to launch coordinated mass attacks on 31 January against 39 of the 44 Provincial capitals, 71 district capitals and 5 of South Vietnam's six autonomous cities, including Saigon. Communist units were alerted to an impending offensive well ahead of time—hence the US intelligence reports—but the timing was not disseminated until 29 January.

The original plan called for the attacks to be launched in the early hours of 30 January, but a 24-hour postponement was ordered at the last moment. The Communist regional command in Viet Cong Military Region 5 failed to get the word, however, and launched attacks in seven cities on 30 January, as planned. This gave all the warning that was needed, but the reports of major attacks were confused, and the prospect of the same thing occurring nationwide 24 hours later seemed incredible.

The opening shots were fired in the city of Nha Trang on the central coast at 12:30 AM on 30 January. Six 82mm mortar rounds were fired at the Vietnamese Navy Training Center, but no injuries were suffered. More than 800 troops of the 18-B North Vietnamese Regiment tried to fight their way into town, but happened to run right into major defenses and were decimated. They never penetrated the town, and their hour-long delay after the mortar attack had allowed South Vietnamese troops to prepare themselves; the NVA attacked at the most likely point, and walked into a major trap. Infiltrators within the city were unable to penetrate any of its previously alerted logistical centers or administrative headquarters. Fierce fighting raged along one edge of the city until dawn, when Communist forces were driven off by the elite 91st Airborne Ranger Battalion of the South Vietnamese Army. The government reported 377 enemy dead and 78 captured, at a cost of 88 South Vietnamese and American troops killed and 220 wounded.

During the same early morning hours, attacks also hit Danang, the second largest city in the country and a major port; Qui Nhon and Hoi An, also major cities on the Central coast; and Pleiku, Kontum, and Ban Me Thuot in the central highlands. In Danang, a battalion of the 2nd North Vietnamese Division had infiltrated the city, and at 2 AM, behind a mortar attack, tried to break into the I Corps headquarters compound just east of the airfield. The defensive forces held, and help soon arrived from South Vietnamese Military Police, US Marine Military Police and a Battalion of South Vietnamese Rangers. The attackers were driven back, and by daylight had disappeared. South and west of the city, however, the main body of the 2nd North Vietnamese Division had been detected as it moved into attack positions. The US 3rd Battalion, 5th Marines, and 2nd Battalion, 3rd Marines, stopped them and brought to bear artillery and air attacks that forced them to retreat. Fighting continued along Highway I south of Danang until the evening of the 31st, but the city was cleared of enemy forces by noon on 30 January.

The other five cities attacked prematurely were actually penetrated by Communist forces, Kontum by three Communist battalions, Qui Nhon by two, and Ban Me Thuot by an unknown number, whose remnants weren't finally driven out of town or killed for two more days.

By ten o'clock Tuesday morning, 30 January, after the night attacks in the northern sections of the country, the US and South Vietnamese Governments had officially cancelled the cease-fire. An order was sent to all US commanders in Vietnam announcing its end and ordering that all American troops be placed on 'maximum alert.' But the result was less than might have been expected: Americans were getting used to alerts after which nothing happened. For all but those troops in the seven cities attacked during the night, it seemed like a case of crying 'wolf.' They did not know that this time, the wolf was at the gates.

For South Vietnamese forces, the situation was worse, if anything. Over half the troops were on some sort of leave to spend the holiday at home, and even President Thieu, who had cancelled the cease-fire, did not bother to return to Saigon from the luxurious vacation home he had built outside his wife's home town of My Tho.

While the top American commanders were prepared for further attacks on 30 and 31 January, no one dreamed of the all-out assault by Communist forces that swept across the nation within the next 24 hours. Some 68,000 Communist troops were committed to the offensive against South Vietnamese and American positions. Although this move was a complete surprise, the attacks were launched primarily against well-established emplacements, with the result that most had suicidal results: nearly all the attacking troops were killed, wounded or captured. It was perhaps no accident that the elite of the South Vietnamese Viet Cong led these attacks, with very little participation by North Vietnamese Army regulars. The result was the massive annihilation of South Vietnamese Communists. (Thus when South Vietnam was welded to North Vietnam as a unified Communist State, the South Vietnamese Communists had no effective military force and were easily excluded from positions of political power.)

When the offensive was launched after midnight on 31 January, most local South Vietnamese forces were successful in quickly defeating the attackers. With the exceptions of Saigon and Hue, Communist forces were soon repulsed in every town they hit.

Known as the 'Paris of the Orient,' Saigon was a city of pleasure and comfort thus far largely untouched by the war. Three million of South Vietnam's 13 million people lived in metropolitan Saigon, and the only military presence felt by most of these inhabitants came from elite troops in tailored fatigues and sunglasses who were continually moved through the city like chess pieces by their commanders—mostly to prepare for or defend against threatened coups d'etat.

In Saigon, life could be comfortable with the help of a little money, which was easy to come by if one were not too particular about the means. It was a seductive setting for American journalists covering the war, many of them young people on their first posts as foreign correspondents. Some ventured no closer toward the sound of the guns, content to rely for their stories on official military briefings, war stories picked up from American soldiers on the street and rumor control. Thus the first news of the Communist Tet Offensive to reach the United States came from Saigon, where the assault exploded at 3:00 AM Wednesday, 31 January. Attacks erupted almost simultaneously at the US Embassy, the Presidential Palace, the government radio station, the headquarters of the US Command and the Vietnamese Joint Generals Staff at Tan Son Nhut Air Base, the Bien Hoa Air Base just outside of town (then the busiest airport in the world), the US III Corps Headquarters in Bien Hoa, and other points throughout the Saigon area.

Because of the proximity of so many American journalists and the political importance of the location, the greatest immediate emphasis was given to the attack on the US Embassy. The first reports, carried by all three television networks and repeated in most newspapers, said that Viet Cong attackers had broken into the Embassy building and seized the first (or several) floors; floor-to-floor fighting reportedly continued, with Communist forces holding the upper hand. In fact, 19 Viet Cong had blown a hole in the eight-foot wall surrounding the Embassy at 3:00 AM and killed two US Military Policemen on guard at the gate. They then attacked the main building —in which only five American soldiers were on duty—but the doors were sealed and despite efforts to blow through the doors, they were unable to do so. Over the next six hours, the compound was counterattacked by US reinforcements. One by one, the Viet Cong were killed in the compound outside the Embassy, with a platoon of paratroopers from the 101st Airborne Division landing on the roof as the last attackers were eliminated. In spite of abundant evidence of a Communist failure, few journalists corrected their original stories; they continued to emphasize the stunning surprise of the attacks and the courage and élan of the attackers. This was a clear example of the way sensationalist journalism sometimes ran amok in reporting the Vietnamese War.

Also at 3:00 AM, a truckload of Viet Cong disguised as South Vietnamese Riot Police arrived at the government radio station. As they pulled up, the guards came out of their bunkers to investigate. They were cut down in a few bursts of gunfire, and hand grenades finished off those who had not come onto the street. The Viet Cong burst into the radio station, accompanied by a North Vietnamese technician who had detailed plans of the station and tapes to air announcing the uprising against the South Vietnamese Government. But this possibility had been anticipated: as the first shots were fired, a technician inside called the transmitter twenty kilometers away and the station was taken off the air. Although the Viet Cong held the facility for six hours, they were never able to use it.

The South Vietnamese Armored and Artillery Commands were located in an open area on the north side of town. They were overrun by two battalions of the 101st Viet Cong Regiment, which planned to use tanks and artillery pieces they would capture there in attacks on other strongpoints in the city. But they found the tanks had been moved the day before, after news of the attacks on the northern cities; the breech blocks had been taken from the howitzers by the defenders before they left, rendering them useless.

General Weyand was the American Commander of the III Corps area, which included Saigon. He was at nearby Bien Hoa, and was one of the senior American commanders who was convinced a Communist attack would be launched before daylight on 31 January in the Saigon area, as the latest intelligence had predicted. Consequently, he was awake when the attacks hit, and by dawn had committed over 5000 American Airborne and mechanized troops in response to reported assaults on US positions.

Tan Son Nhut Air Base was hit hard from three directions.

Two battalions of the 9th Viet Cong division soon managed to burst through the western defenses, but two companies of South Vietnamese Airborne troops and the American Security Force counterattacked as they reached the buildings and stopped them despite heavy casualties. A US armored cavalry troop of tanks from the 25th Infantry Division came crashing in behind the Viet Cong, striking them from the rear and scattering the survivors.

Bien Hoa Air Base and the III Corps Headquarters compound where General Weyand was managing his troops were hit by a heavy rocket attack followed by a ground attack. The air base was hit by the 274th Viet Cong Regiment, and the III Corps Headquarters Compound by the 275th Viet Cong Regiment. The 274th managed to break through the barbed-wire defenses and had reached the hangars and the USAF Hospital and office buildings when they were hit by helicopter gunships firing rockets and machine guns; this broke the back of the attack and scattered the VC soldiers. A counterattack by elements of the 199th Light Infantry Brigade routed the survivors as daylight arrived. The 275th Regiment was mowed down by defenders at III Corps Headquarters Compound and never entered the installation.

The Presidential Palace, which was always filled with South Vietnamese troops armed to the teeth, was hit by 13 men and a woman, who attempted to drive a truck filled with explosives through a side gate, but were repelled by alert guards. They took refuge in nearby buildings, but all were eventually killed or captured.

The heavily Chinese suburb of Cholon was invaded by several Viet Cong Battalions during the night, but since they neither attacked nor occupied any government or American positions there, they were largely ignored for several days. Several Viet Cong Battalions dug positions in the Phu Tho Race Track area. When South Vietnamese Airborne and Ranger troops began a house-to-house search of Cholon on 2 February, numerous firefights erupted. Allied air and artillery support destroyed much of Cholon thereafter, but the final Communist resistance at the race track wasn't snuffed out until 9 February. Most other Communist resistance in the

Saigon area had been eliminated by 2 February, but when Cholon was finally cleared, all enemy troops in III Corps who had participated in the Tet Offensive had been destroyed or routed.

The Communists had committed 35 battalions to the Tet Offensive in III Corps, and 11 battalions to Saigon itself. Many of the soldiers had slipped into town on 29 or 30 January in civilian dress and gathered at safe houses, where they were issued weapons and ammunition. Other Communist units never reached their targets. The 4th Battalion of the 165-A Viet Cong Regiment, for example, had been ordered to attack the main Saigon prison and free its 6000 inmates, many of whom were Communists. On the way there, they were discovered and fired upon by South Vietnamese police. A major battle followed with a company of South Vietnamese Rangers alerted by the gunfire, and they never reached the prison.

Even those units who did reach their targets were poorly deployed. Multiple battalions were used to attack major installations like air bases, but too many other targets were hit by forces too small to take them or, if surprise was complete, to hold them for any significant period of time. The Communist leadership seemed to think that the South Vietnamese Government and military were very frail organizations, needing only the slightest jolt to collapse them. They also believed that the South Vietnamese population was seething under oppression, ready to rise and join the Communists in the overthrow of their oppressors at the first opportunity. But in the event, such expectations were to be dashed by a viable governmental and military establishment and a secure, contented populace. The Communist Tet Offensive was quickly repelled in Saigon and elsewhere throughout the country, in most cases within 24 hours.

Meanwhile, in the population centers of the northernmost I Corps—with the exception of Hue—the Communist offensive met the same response it had found in Saigon. But because of their proximity to North Vietnam, attacks on northern cities like Quang Tri were of particular importance. North of Hue and only some 20 kilometers south of the DMZ, Quang Tri lies on the east bank of the Thach Han River, 10 kilometers from the sea. By the 30th of January, the Communists had infiltrated the 10th Sapper Battalion into Quang Tri City. The Sappers began their internal attack at 2:00 AM on 31 January, but supportive attacks from outside by the 812th North Vietnamese Regiment did not occur until two hours later. The enemy attacks were launched from the north, south and east, but the South Vietnamese 1st Regiment and 9th Airborne Battalion defending the city had been alerted by the earlier Sapper attacks. The K-4 Battalion of the 812th Regiment attacked from the east and penetrated the defenses, hoping to capture the Province Headquarters compound and the artillery unit located there, and occupy the city prison. The K-6 Battalion hit from the south and tried to overrun the La Vang South Vietnamese army base in that area of the city. The K-8 Battalion and the 814th Viet Cong Battalion struck the city from the north, while the K-5 Battalion was held in reserve to the southeast of town.

All Communist attacks met blistering fire from the defenders, but they continued to move into the city. The battle was still raging at noon on the 31st when two battalions of the US 1st Cavalry Division landed east of town and hit the enemy from the rear. That crushed the Communist attack, and by nightfall, enemy forces had broken contact and escaped to the north and south of town.

Throughout the rest of I and II Corps, the attacks on towns launched on the 30th and 31st were all blunted and driven off within 48 hours—again, with the exception of Hue. But North Vietnamese and Viet Cong forces continued to launch mortar and rocket attacks against logistical centers and cut road traffic with spoiling raids and small-arms fire for weeks to come. While the population centers were secure, travel was hazardous, and would remain so for some time to come.

Down in the Delta, the populous IV Corps area of the country, the attack was basically the same: sudden and ferocious, but disorganized and undermanned. The city of My Tho was attacked by the 261st, 263rd and 514th Viet Cong Battalions; Ben Tre by the 308th and 306th Viet Cong Battalions; Vinh Long by the 857th and 304th Viet Cong Battalions; Cai Lay by the 261st Viet Cong Battalion and the

540th and 530th Viet Cong District Companies. These assaults were driven off by the South Vietnamese 9th and 21st Divisions, South Vietnamese Ranger and Marine Battalions, elements of the US 9th Infantry Division and South Vietnamese regional forces. The Viet Cong did not hold any position for more than 48 hours, although allied and artillery strikes did considerable damage to populated areas. Large portions of Ben Tre, for instance, were reduced to rubble, giving rise to the famous report by an American advisor, 'We had to destroy the town in order to save it.'

By 3 February 1968, all the Tet Offensive attacks had been essentially stopped and the attackers driven off except in parts of Saigon and Hue. The Communists had taken an enormous gamble, and paid a high price to do so: estimates of their losses during the few days of hot combat ranged from 35,000 to 50,000. But the popular uprising they had predicted to their troops and tried to foment in the general populace never took place. Similarly, no South Vietnamese troops came over to the Communist side, not a single unit of any size: they stood up very well to the challenge, holding to their defenses and repelling the attacks almost everywhere.

The Communist side lost much credibility to the average South Vietnamese citizen: an all-out assault made in the middle of the biggest national holiday, when the government and military were at their most relaxed, had failed miserably. Within days government control was re-established everywhere. If they had been unable to win an offensive of this kind, it seemed improbable that they could ever win. Also, the lack of a popular uprising despite exhortations by the Communist invaders, coupled with their brutal mass murder of civilians during brief periods when they gained control, gave new stature to the South Vietnamese Government. People who had opposed it before changed their attitudes, and voluntary enlistments in the military to fight Communist forces went up after Tet.

The South Vietnamese lost 3000 killed and 8000 wounded, while the American tallies were 1500 killed and 7500 wounded during that brief period. Perhaps 10,000 South Vietnamese civilians were killed in crossfires, and thousands more are known to have been murdered by Communist occupying forces. Nearly a million citizens were made homeless or suffered serious damage to their homes and possessions as a result of the Communist onslaught, and it was clear to the common man where the blame for this lay.

But the most important outcome of the Tet Offensive of 1968 was political, and it took place in the United States, in the minds of the American people and their leaders. As the offensive unfolded, it was reported to them by American print and broadcast journalists: almost everything the Communists did was reported in grandiose style, while reports that came from the South Vietnamese or the American military were treated cynically, as if they were fabrications. When General Westmoreland publicly announced, within a few days, that the Tet Offensive had been a major defeat for the Communists and a major victory for allied forces—a fact obvious to anyone who viewed the events dispassionately—he was treated like a self-deluding fool by the news media.

While many media respresentatives continued to trumpet Tet as a major Communist victory despite the facts, a certain amount of disillusionment had certainly been orchestrated by President Johnson's White House. The American public, having heard for months that the Communists were near defeat and allied forces in the ascendancy all over South Vietnam, found this sudden mammoth attack difficult to reconcile with such glowing reports. The fact that the Communist attacks were actually suicidal never became clear until it was far too late to matter.

The Communist Tet Offensive of 1968 marked the beginning of the decision by American leaders to disengage themselves from a war in which they were unbeatable on the field of battle, but which they never clearly understood.

American infantrymen jumping from a UH-1D ("Huey")
heliocopter into combat.

Tay Ninh, Vietnam. A gun crew prepares to fire a 175mm gun at Communist positions during Operation Junction City.

South Vietnam....A U.S. Air Force F-100 Supersabre aircraft fires folding-fin rockets into an enemy position. The F-100s have been bombing and strafing enemy positions while supporting U.S. and allied units in South Vietnam. The Supersabres are equipped with bombs, rockets, and cannon.

UH-1D "Huey" helicopters from the 173rd Aviation Company, 11th Combat Aviation Battalion, fly in formation in preparation for a combat insertion of infantry troops.

An American river Patrol boat leaves the dock at Go Dau Ha, Vietnam.

Artillery barges of the Riverine Force, 9th Infantry Division, are beached on the My Tho River to offload equipment.

American infantrymen attempt to advance on an enemy position while under hostile fire.

An aerial view of the Old Imperial Palace in Hue which was held by communist forces during the 1968 Tet Offensive.

An aerial view of the U.S. Marine Corps fortress at Khe Sanh after surviving the Communist siege during January and February of 1968.

An American infantry patrol moves out in their typical single file formation in search of the enemy.

American helicopters support the Vietnamese troops participating in Operation Lam Son 719.

American helicopters support South Vietnamese forces as they fought to stem the Communist Easter Offensive of 1972.

RETAKING THE CITADEL

The Battle of Hue

The last few days of January 1968 saw the smooth secretive infiltration of Communist troops wearing civilian garb into downtown Hue. Their weapons and ammunition were easily transported in wagons, truck beds and other hiding places; in the holiday mood that prevailed, little attention was paid to the unusually large number of hard-looking young soldiers in the boisterous throngs. After all, the ceasefire had been declared by both sides, and many South Vietnamese troops were officially released from duty and relaxing with their families and friends.

Of all the towns and cities in South Vietnam, none was more naturally suited to seizure by a quick armed attack and subsequent defense against strong counterattacks than was Hue. The third largest city in South Vietnam, Hue is bisected by the Perfume (Huong) River flowing through it from the southwest and on to the ocean some twelve kilometers away. On the north bank lies the Citadel, a walled city within a city. The Citadel contains the ancient Imperial Palace, from which the former state of Annam—which covered most of the central portion of present-day Vietnam—was once ruled. It is some three square kilometers in area and encloses roughly two-thirds of Hue. The other third lies on the south of the river, the two sections being joined by a railroad bridge and the Nguyen Hoang bridge, over which the major north-south

Route 1 passes. The Citadel has long been protected by the diverted river on all four sides, and a complex moat and massive stone walls also insulate it from any potential attackers. There were no American units inside the Citadel, and the only South Vietnamese military presence there was the headquarters of the 1st Division, Army of the Republic of Vietnam, sandwiched against the northeast corner.

As a result of the numerous Tet truce violations by Communist forces, US and South Vietnamese military commanders officially ended the cease-fire on 30 January. The Commander of the 1st ARVN Division, General Ngo Quang Truong, called his men back to their units, and on 30 January his headquarters was on full alert. The enemy attack came at about 3:30 in the morning of 31 January in the form of a rocket and mortar barrage, followed by a ground assault by ten Viet Cong and North Vietnamese battalions. They quickly took virtually all of Hue south of the river, and the great bulk of Hue on the north bank, including the Citadel except for the 1st Division headquarters. The 100-percent alert meant that the entire Division staff was there, as well as some American Advisors. Most importantly, the Hac Bao or Black Panther Company, an elite all-volunteer unit that served as the Division Reaction Force, was also well prepared: with the staff members, they were able to stave off repeated Communist attacks.

Several pockets of resistance held out against the initial ground attack in the city south of the river, including the American Advisory headquarters at the Military Assistance Command Vietnam compound. After the rocket and mortar attack, the 804th Battalion and other elements of the 4th North Vietnamese Division hit the northeast corner of the compound, but were repelled by quickly assembled American defenders armed with individual weapons. The North Vietnamese launched a second attack against the southeast corner just before dawn, but this, too, was beaten off with small-arms fire. The American defenders sent out radio alarms along with calls for heavier weapons and troop support. The rest of Hue south of the river was by now controlled by units of the 4th North Vietnamese Regiment. Because of the city's dense population, it was initially decided not to use artillery or air strikes, though later developments would allow exceptions to this rule.

To the north, most of the Citadel had been quickly taken by the 800th and 802nd Battalions of the 6th North Vietnamese Regiment. Around 4:00 AM, the 800th was blocked at the Hue city airport inside the Citadel by the Hac Bao Company, and quickly moved to the south; while this was happening, the 802nd had penetrated the 1st ARVN Division compound. The Hac Bao Company was quickly brought back to headquarters, and together with the 200-man division staff managed to drive the enemy out of the division headquarters area. But by dawn the entire Citadel, save only the 1st ARVN Division headquarters compound, was controlled by the two Battalions of the 6th NVA Regiment, reinforced by the 12th NVA Sapper Battalion.

First light saw only two major pockets of resistance remaining in all of Hue: the 1st ARVN Division compound in the north and the MAC-V compound in the south. But for them, things looked grim. There were other, smaller groups of ARVN soldiers but they were surrounded and cut off from each other—most of them just 'played possum.'

Meanwhile, American and South Vietnamese forces had been deployed at once to the rescue. General Truong ordered a regiment of the 1st ARVN Airborne Task Force—elite paratroopers—and a troop of ARVN Armored Cavalry to move to the Citadel; the US 1st Marine Division sent elements of the 1st Marine regiment. But the North Vietnamese had established blocking positions outside the city to stop any US or ARVN reinforcements. The 806th NVA Battalion blocked Highway 1 northwest of Hue, while the 804th NVA Battalion and the K4B Battalion with elements of another sapper battalion were in southern Hue. The 810th Battalion was blocking Highway 1 south of Hue.

Early that morning A Company, 1st Battalion, 1st Marines and G Company, 2nd Battalion, 5th Marines were sent north to Hue from Phu Bai by truck to rescue the MAC-V compound. They picked up a platoon of tanks on the way, and in spite of heavy resistance were able to blast their way through to a beleagured band of Advisors by three that afternoon. They were then ordered across the river in an effort to reach the 1st ARVN Division headquarters within the Citadel. With the help of the firepower provided by the tanks, they managed to cross the mammoth stone bridge, but at great cost. Once on the north side, however, they were unable to breach the walls of the Citadel; they withdrew to the MAC-V compound on the southern side of the river.

Two battalions of the ARVN Airborne as well as the Armored Cavalry troop managed to fight their way to the 1st ARVN Division headquarters on the 31st, while two battalions of the 3rd ARVN Regiment began moving toward the Citadel from the west on the northern side of the river. It was decided that ARVN forces would be responsible for clearing Communist forces from the Citadel and the rest of Hue north of the river, while American forces would assume the same responsibility for the southern side.

On 1 February both ARVN forces and US Marines began offensive operations in their assigned areas. From the very start, it was messy, dirty work—house-to-house fighting through city streets—of a type unseen by Americans since World War II. On 2 February a brigade of the 1st Cavalry (airmobile) began sealing off Hue City to the west and north; they would later be joined by elements of the 101st Airborne Division on the southern flank. While these US Army units saw plenty of action in the outlying areas, the grim city fighting was to remain largely in the hands of South Vietnamese troops and US Marines.

On 2 February the weather also took a turn for the worse: temperatures plummeted into the fifties, and the clouds opened up and dumped a constant bone-chilling rain on the combatants. The low cloud cover made accurate tactical air support virtually impossible, and even artillery fire was often adjusted by sound when the flashes were swallowed by the gray blanket.

By 11 February less than half the Citadel had been recovered from Communist forces. Re-supplies and reinforcements reached them each night from the west and north, or even on boats coming down the river. On 10 February two battalions of the US 101st Airborne Division were brought into the fray south of the river. The next day two reinforced ARVN battalions succeeded in retaking the airfield inside the Citadel, and on 12 February the 4th and 9th ARVN Airborne Battalions landed there from Dong Ha and Quang Tri.

On the south of the river, the Marines had recovered the Province headquarters, the jail and the hospital by 6 February; by 9 February most enemy resistance had been crushed. The bodies of 1053 Communist soldiers were recovered, and control of that sector of the city was returned to the South Vietnamese Government.

On 12 February the 1st Battalion 5th US Marines made a combat assault into the Citadel by helicopter. There they joined South Vietnamese Marines, Airborne Battalions and the 1st ARVN Division in slugging it out with growing numbers of Communist forces who were reinforced and supplied nightly. From 13 to 22 February the battle swayed back and forth while much of the city was pounded to rubble by artillery from both sides. On 19 February the US 1st Cavalry (airmobile) was able to move up to and seal off the western wall of the Citadel, thus depriving the North Vietnamese of smoothly flowing reinforcements and supplies. This quickly sapped the Communist will to fight, and on the night of 23–24 February, the 2nd Battalion 3rd ARVN Regiment launched a surprise flanking night attack along the southeastern wall of the Citadel. The North Vietnamese were caught off guard and forced to withdraw. By dawn the South Vietnamese flag had replaced the Viet Cong banner that had flown from the Citadel flagpole for 25 days. The last Communist positions were quickly abandoned or overrun, and the remnants of the Communist forces in Hue slipped away or were killed.

The battle of Hue had been particularly bitter. Ten North Vietnamese and Viet Cong battalions defended from strong positions against eleven South Vietnamese battalions, three US Marine battalions and four US Army battalions, supported by American air and artillery which, because of the dense civilian population around the enemy positions, could not often be used effectively. The Communists paid a heavy price—5000 of their soldiers killed in the city and another 3000 in nearby engagements. But the greatest suffering was borne by the South Vietnamese civilians. Some 116,000 were made homeless by this action, which also saw the death or disappearance of 5800 others. Over the ensuing year, fresh mass graves were found throughout the formerly occupied areas of Hue containing over 2800 bodies, many with their hands tied behind their backs. The victims had been taken away by Communist political officers and shot or bludgeoned to death. Others were simply buried alive. Captured Communist documents gave disturbingly broad reasons for these murders: victims included those who had served in the South Vietnamese military, government functionaries, policemen, doctors, religious leaders, professors, political leaders, and troublesome foreigners—European medical personnel and missionaries—whose governments were not there to defend them. For the surviving populace of Hue, it would seem fortunate that they were rescued from such arbitrary violence after only 26 days.

THE MARINE CORPS HOLDS

The Battle of Khe Sanh

As American Advisors arrived in South Vietnam during the early 1960s, one of their main efforts was directed at impeding the flow of troops and supplies from North Vietnam. For this effort, a series of fortified strong points was established just south of the Demilitarized Zone, from which indigenous forces could launch spoiling attacks against the main routes of infiltration.

The westernmost of these bases was established on the Khe Sanh plateau some 25 kilometers south of the Demilitarized Zone and 16 kilometers east of the Laotian border. The US Army Special Forces built a camp there around an old French airfield, which was ideally located for staging attacks by the South Vietnamese Civilian Irregular Defense Group (CIDG), which they advised.

In 1966 a US Marine contingent took over the camp and the Special Forces moved closer to Laos and built another camp at Lang Vei. The runway was lengthened and strengthened to accommodate major US air transports, and the Marines regularly sent patrols to clear the surrounding hills. In April 1967 one such patrol hit a major North Vietnamese force near Hill 861 and found many carefully constructed positions showing North Vietnamese intentions to besiege Khe Sanh.

The American reaction was to send in two battalions of

the 3rd Marines and clear hills 861, 881N and 881S. Soon thereafter, the three battalions of the 26th Marines replaced the 3rd Marines. American commanders believed the North Vietnamese would attack Khe Sanh; it was an inviting target, and if allowed to remain in place, might significantly disrupt the movement of Communist supplies and reinforcements south. Intelligence reports indicated that the North Vietnamese 325C Division was assembling just north of the combat base, and the 304th Division was nearby to the southwest. In addition to the 20,000 enemy troops these two divisions could muster, the 324th and 320th Divisions were less than 25 kilometers away and could be brought into battle in short order. It was also noted that these particular units were lavishly supplied with artillery, mortars and rockets of all sizes and descriptions, and it was expected that all this firepower would be brought to bear on the Marine combat base at Khe Sanh.

Confronted with this situation, General Westmoreland's choices were to withdraw his forces and concede the area to the North Vietnamese, or to hold on to this key base on the jugular of so much Communist infiltration into South Vietna? In a key strategic move, he elected to hold, thus challenging the Communists much as they had been challenged by the French at Dien Bien Phu in 1954. In the fall of 1967 massive US air power had crushed enemy forces that besieged another Marine base at Con Thien, and Westmoreland directed his staff, in early January 1968, to plan a similar defense for Khe Sanh, relying primarily on air power rather than a large number of American troops.

The physical size of the base at Khe Sanh precluded the presence of more than about 6000 men in any case. The three battalions of the 26th Marines as well as the 1st Battalion, 13th Marines, were in place by early January 1968. One Marine artillery battalion of 18 105mm howitzers was located at Khe Sanh, as were six larger 155mm guns. There were also 175mm guns at other bases that were located within their 32-kilometer range which could provide support when needed. Finally, there were six M-48 tanks mounting 90mm guns; ten Ontos tracked antitank vehicles, each mounting six

106mm recoilless rifles, and four 'Dusters,' tracked vehicles mounting clusters of either 40mm guns or 50-caliber machine guns. In addition to these heavy weapons, the defenders were armed with individual and crew-served weapons, and were, by mid-January, formidably entrenched. Sand-bagged bunkers and trenches were everywhere, and the perimeter was protected by heavily mined and intricately fashioned barbed-wire defenses. The commanders were also mindful of the Dien Bien Phu precedent, and had established rock-ribbed outposts atop several of the neighboring hills to prevent the North Vietnamese from using them to dominate the American fortress. If the enemy wanted a fight, he would find one here.

Soon after midnight on 21 January, the North Vietnamese launched their long-awaited attack. Mortar shells hammered the Marine outpost on Hill 861, and a ground attack soon followed as sappers—individual soldiers carrying explosive charges—blasted their way through the barbed wire for waves of infantry that followed them. While some attackers did get through the wire, they were killed by defending troops as well as by fire directed on them from another Marine outpost on the higher ground of nearby Hill 881S, which the North Vietnamese surprisingly ignored during their attack.

After having been repulsed on Hill 861, the Communists turned their fire on the main Khe Sanh base. Just before dawn, mortar and artillery shells as well as rockets began pounding the American fortifications. One round found the largest ammunition dump and blew nearly 1500 tons of ammo in a thunderous explosion. A flurry of aerial activity followed this attack, and massive air strikes, including B-52 raids, pummeled the surrounding hills, touching off many secondary explosions and fires.

The Senior Officer on the ground was Colonel Lownds, Commander of the 26th Marines, and he was suddenly confronted with enormous challenges even while his men were under fire: foremost was ensuring that enough ammunition replaced that lost in the first major barrage to enable the fortress to hold against the enemy attack. This was no simple task, as the airstrip had been so heavily damaged that only the smaller C-123 transports could land safely. But an emergency call brought together enough of these aircraft to land some 130 tons of ammunition by nightfall on the 22nd. On that day, the 1st Battalion, 9th Marines arrived at Khe Sanh, and Colonel Lownds placed them around a rock quarry west of the base. He also extended his string of outposts, from Hill 950 across the Rao Quan River to Hill 881S. On 27 January he received his last reinforcements, the South Vietnamese 37th Ranger Battalion, which took over the defense of a portion of the perimeter.

Another problem was created by the arrival of refugees at the Marine base. Initially, some civilians were flown out on cargo planes that had been offloaded, but soon the press of civilians and irregular troops became unmanageable. The willingness to safeguard human life had to be balanced against the limited space, the danger from hostile fire and the threat of enemy infiltration. While the Communist bombardment of the base continued through the last week of January, so did the responding American artillery fire and air strikes. Between attacks, repairs were made to the airstrip so that the heavy C-130 transports were able to land again, and supplies were heavily stockpiled.

The enemy had deployed a major infantry force around Khe Sanh, complete with artillery and anti-aircraft guns. He had begun to build bunkers and dig trenchworks that would be needed in the expected major assault, and Communist tanks were sighted to the west and south of the US base, clearly threatening the intention to plow through American defenses. Everyone from the newest Marine private in the trenches to the President of the United States expected the next move to be a major human-wave assault against the Khe Sanh base, and they were ready for it.

But the attack that came on 31 January was the Tet Offensive, directed against the cities and towns of South Vietnam rather than at US bases. While no major ground attack was yet hurled against the main camp at Khe Sanh, the pressure never lessened: heavy enemy artillery bombardments became the norm. Major attacks on 5 February again tried to take the Marine outposts on Hills 881S and 861A, but with the support of artillery and air strikes, they were beaten back.

The American defenders appeared—and felt—secure in

their defensive bulwark, but on 7 February the nearby Special Forces camp at Lang Vei was hit and eventually overrun by North Vietnamese forces. In spite of excellent supporting defenses, the tool that won the day for the Communists was a dozen or so PT-76 Russian-built tanks. While a number of the tanks had been destroyed during the battle, they ultimately overwhelmed the defenses at Lang Vei and sent the surviving American Special Forces and their CIDG troops streaming toward Khe Sanh in headlong retreat.

When the retreating troops reached the base, they were met by some grim Marines, who expected to be hit by major artillery-supported infantry attacks. The sudden appearance of enemy tanks made things look still worse for a 6000-man garrison in the middle of nowhere surrounded by some 40,000 hungry enemy soldiers.

The Lang Vei camp had fallen on the morning of 8 February, after more than 24 hours of intense fighting. Fourteen of the 24 American Special Forces soldiers made it to safety at Khe Sanh, and hundreds of their surviving indigenous troops came streaming through the jungle after them. As they sought to enter the base, the Marines were confronted again with the limitations of space, physical danger from Communist fire and the threat of enemy infiltration. Finally, it was decided to disarm these irregular troops and hold them outside the perimeter until the Green Berets could sort through them and designate the genuine CIDG members eligible for evacuation by air.

On 9 February a major North Vietnamese attack hit an outpost several hundred meters west of the rock quarry held by the 1st of the 9th Marines. Although ground was lost in the dark, a fierce Marine counterattack after dawn drove the enemy from the field. While the Americans had lost 21 killed within a few short hours, they counted 134 North Vietnamese bodies on the battlefield. That was to be the last major ground attack for some two weeks, but the North Vietnamese redoubled their classic siege efforts—long, deep trenches incorporating zig-zags, mining, tunneling—a very complex and sophisticated engineering operation that brought the Communists ever closer to the American defenses.

But tactical air support flown by US Air Force, Navy and

Marine fighters pounded the enemy positions that now ringed the Khe Sanh base. Farther out, B-52 strikes literally pulverized the ground, grinding everything and everyone below them into powder. The round-the-clock bombing operation, appropriately named 'Niagara,' was beginning to turn the once-heavily jungled countryside around Khe Sanh into a wasted, uninhabitable moonscape.

On 11 February two large C-130 cargo aircraft were hit as they landed at Khe Sanh. One of them was quickly engulfed in flame and soon burned to a hulk, immolating six crew members in the process. The other was quickly jury-rigged to take off again and limped to Danang, where mechanics counted 242 holes in the transport after it landed. It was quickly decided that the limited number of C-130 transports available were a 'make-or-break' resource too valuable to squander by risking them on the ground at Khe Sanh. From 12 February until the end of March, C-130s landed there on only four days, although they continued to drop resupplies on the base by parachute. Most of their slack was taken up by increased use of the smaller, lighter C-123, which needed less time and runway to take off and was a much smaller risk on the ground at Khe Sanh.

In spite of the breathtaking volume of ordnance being dumped on them, the North Vietnamese continued their artillery barrage and small-arms fire unabated. On 23 February over 1300 shells pounded the Marine base, a record for one day. One of them hit an ammunition dump, and blew up more than 1500 American artillery rounds, causing a series of explosions that shook the entire camp repeatedly. The trenches could now be seen reaching within one or two hundred meters of the perimeter at dawn, having progressed as much as 100 meters during a single night. Rumors on the base said the North Vietnamese were tunneling under them and would burst out of the ground in their midst even as their comrades on the outside rushed the barbed wire.

But this never occurred. The only attack on the perimeter came against the sector held by the South Vietnamese 37th Ranger Battalion in the early morning hours of 1 March. As the Communists rushed the perimeter, they were met by a hail of flesh-shredding hand grenades, bursting claymore mines and automatic-weapons fire. The attackers got no farther than the masses of barbed wire surrounding the perimeter, leaving 70 bodies enmeshed there as mute testimony of their futile effort.

After 1 March the seasonal weather change began to arrive in the area. Clouded, rainy days and nights that limited tactical air support began to give way to dry, sunny periods and skies literally filled with American aircraft. Even with intensified bombing of North Vietnamese positions, March was an uneasy month for the Marines at Khe Sanh. On two occasions, intelligence resources alerted the base to be prepared for major ground attacks.

On 13 March—the 14th anniversary of the beginning of the siege at Dien Bien Phu—the massing of North Vietnamese troops and munitions, apparently for an assault, caused an immediate strong reaction from US artillery and air forces. On the 14th B-52 crews reported 59 secondary explosions from their bombs, and North Vietnamese bodies littered an apparent assembly area only two kilometers outside the wire. Another attack seemed to be massing on 21–22 March, and another Marine ammunition dump was hit by a hostile shell, temporarily ending much of the artillery fire going out of Khe Sanh.

An AC-47 gunship appeared overhead that night along with other tactical aircraft, and the threat of a North Vietnamese ground attack quickly diminished. The AC-47 'Spooky,' one of the old two-engine DC-3 transports, flies in a slow, steady curve several thousand feet up when used tactically. It is equipped with precise instrumentation that allows its exact location to be fed continuously by computers to its fire stations; armament consists of six Gatling guns whose fire is directed downward from an open cargo door in its side. Each of these guns is capable of firing 6000 20mm rounds per minute, and the big, lumbering aircraft can carry a lot of ammunition. Every sixth round is a red tracer, and when Spooky is firing, particularly at night, it appears that a giant hand is pouring molten lead from a pitcher in the sky. It is an eerie and frightening sight.

On 23 March more than 1000 North Vietnamese artillery rounds hit the defenses at Khe Sanh, but again the barrages were not followed by the expected ground attack, undoubtedly because of the massive US air support: B-52s reported detonating 88 secondary explosions during strikes they made that day.

Throughout the siege—which would last from 21 January until the beginning of April—the 6000 men at Khe Sanh bases were resupplied exclusively by air. During the siege of Dien Bien Phu in 1954, the French had managed to drop an average of 100 tons of supplies each day to their beleagured garrison, and few aircraft could land to embark dead or wounded. By way of contrast, the American garrison at Khe Sanh, which numbered roughly half the French force at Dien Bien Phu, received around 300 tons of supplies by air each day. While the runway was kept repaired and transports could land and take off, much of the re-supply was effected by lower-risk parachute drops. The strong Marine outposts on the surrounding hills were themselves surrounded by powerful enemy forces and depended exclusively on helicopters for resupply. Since these outposts were of company or smaller size, this presented little problem, although there were some tense moments when ammunition supplies ran low during North Vietnamese assaults on their positions. One of the key reasons that Khe Sanh survived the siege is clearly the fact that none of these outposts were ever taken by the Communists; despite their major efforts, the Americans held fast to the hilltops dominating the base.

By the end of March, it was clear that the North Vietnamese were withdrawing troops from the siege. The Americans planned a major relief effort, Operation Pegasus, with the 1st Regiment, 1st Marines slated to to clear Highway 9 to the Khe Sanh base. Simultaneously, the 1st Cavalry Division (Airmobile) was to establish fire bases on either side of Highway 9 from which artillery support could be extended to the attacking Marines.

Just after dawn on 30 March, B Company of the 1st Battalion, 26th Marines ventured out from the perimeter, carefully taking advantage of a friendly artillery barrage and early-morning fog, and plunged into a major North Vietnamese assembly area. The enemy, totally surprised, took refuge in bunkers, but the raiders followed them with flame throwers, satchel charges, grenades and small-arms fire, killing an estimated 150 Communist soldiers before returning to their lines.

On 1 April Operation Pegasus was launched, but met surprisingly light resistance. Prisoners taken confirmed intelligence reports that only the North Vietnamese 304th Division remained in the area. That same day, the 1st Battalion 9th Marines stormed a hill some 2500 meters south of the Khe Sanh airstrip, and later that day repulsed a Communist counterattack. Things began to move quickly now, and Operation Pegasus was storming to the rescue virtually unopposed. On 6 April a battalion of the 1st Cavalry relieved the 1st of the 9th Marines, and a few days later the 3rd Brigade of the 1st Cavalry assumed responsibility for the defense of the Khe Sanh base, relieving the beleagured Marines and South Vietnamese Rangers.

Operation Pegasus continued until 15 April, by which time American and South Vietnamese troops had recovered control of northwestern Quang Tri Province, including the site of the Lang Vei Special Forces camp. Occasional mortar attacks still occurred, but the enemy troop masses that once besieged the Khe Sanh base had disappeared. The Marine contingent stationed there was reduced to around a thousand men, while the rest of the garrison was formed into a mobile task force to be used throughout western Quang Tri.

The structures at Khe Sanh were finally dismantled and the base was closed in June 1968. Brigadier General Carl W Hoffman, who commanded the mobile task force, said that emphasis was changing from static defense to a more flexible operation. 'We have not abandoned our interest in the Khe Sanh plateau,' he said. 'What we have abandoned is the sandbagged island in the middle of it.'

Comparison with Dien Bien Phu cannot be avoided, and in both cases the siege and prolonged battle were of political as well as military importance. Had Khe Sanh fallen to the Communists as Dien Bien Phu had, the Americans might well have ended their presence in Vietnam much earlier than they did. The major variation was heavy use of air and artillery support by the Americans, which, if available, clearly would have changed the situation for the French 14 years earlier. Close to 200,000 mortar and artillery shells were fired in defense of Khe Sanh, and the well-named Operation Niagara brought more than 100,000 tons of bombs raining down on the North Vietnamese from aircraft of all descriptions. From 20 January to 31 March, 199 Americans were killed while manning Khe Sanh's defenses; some 1600 were wounded. Although no body count of enemy dead was possible, General Westmoreland's systems analysis office prepared four mathematical models showing that the North Vietnamese suffered between 9800 and 13,000 men killed or seriously wounded.

Khe Sanh held; Dien Bien Phu did not. Both were important psychological points, major contests of the force of wills between two governments. Given the enormous size of the attacking force, Khe Sanh proved again the great strength of a confident, well-prepared defense—particularly when it can afford to spend ten tons of of bombs and twenty artillery rounds for each attacker killed.

THE CAMBODIAN INCURSION

By 1970, most of South Vietnam was firmly under the control of the South Vietnamese Government, and Communist forces avoided contact with allied forces. Only in northernmost I Corps were the Communists willing to engage in combat: in II, III and IV Corps, they had been largely driven back to the Cambodian border area. The American effort to 'Vietnamize' the war was well under way, and troop units amounting to over 100,000 US soldiers had returned to the United States. Over 47,000 Communist troops had 'rallied' to the South Vietnamese side during 1969, and the South Vietnamese force structure had swelled to more than 950,000 soldiers. Clearly, the Communists were losing the war.

Meanwhile, dramatic changes were taking place in Cambodia. There had been a sizable ethnic spillover between these two countries over the last several hundred and even thousands of years: in 1970, around 500,000 ethnic Cambodians lived in South Vietnam, while some 400,000 ethnic Vietnamese lived in Cambodia. Whatever the formal rules of citizenship were, the ethnic bonds have always been the tightest, and the inherited tensions between these groups periodically erupted into brutally savage rampages, which neither government could or would prevent.

Prince Sihanouk, the Cambodian ruler, had broken diplomatic relations with South Vietnam in August 1963, and with the United States in May 1965, and declared Cambodia's neutrality. However, he had preserved peace for his country by allowing the North Vietnamese Communist forces to use his territory for transit of supplies and reinforcements into South Vietnam. There were two main routes used for this: the Ho Chi Minh Trail, which ran south through Laos and Cambodia just west of the South Vietnamese border; and the Cambodian port of Kompong Som (renamed 'Sihanoukville' under Prince Sihanouk's rule), where heavy cargo ships in the service of North Vietnam or her allies were able to discharge their freight for trans-shipment by Communist forces to the South Vietnamese border area. Naturally, since the middle 1960s the Communists had, as a practical measure, established vast support and service areas just inside Cambodia, from which they were able to supply and manage the war in South Vietnam with complete safety. Cambodia's status as an independent 'neutral' nation had precluded, before 1970, any military attack by either South Vietnam or the United States on these 'safe' Communist rear areas.

By March of 1970, however, the unpopular North Vietnamese military presence in Cambodia began to produce dramatic displays of distress by the indigenous population. From 8 to 10 March, massive demonstrations took place in the Cambodian provinces along the South Vietnamese border, demanding that North Vietnamese troops and support forces leave Cambodia. In Pnom Penh, outraged crowds marched on the North Vietnamese Embassy, hurling rocks and obscenities through its windows. Sihanouk was in France for medical treatment, and General Lon Nol was acting as the Head of Government in his absence. On 12 March he demanded that Hanoi withdraw all North Vietnamese forces from Cambodia by 15 March. Four days later more anticommunist demonstrations occurred across the country, and on 18 March, the Cambodian National Assembly stripped Sihanouk of all governmental powers, and Lon Nol took over as Prime Minister.

On 25 and 26 March, there were demonstrations in favor of Sihanouk in some provinces, and the new Cambodian Government used troops to disperse the crowds. In early April the North Vietnamese began to attack Cambodian army posts, and the old ethnic rivalries resurfaced. The Cambodian Government published orders for Vietnamese residents to assemble in camps and abide by restrictive curfews. On 15 April hundreds of bodies of Vietnamese were found in the Mekong River, hands bound behind their backs, floating downstream into South Vietnam from the direction of Pnom Penh. On 17 April, the new Cambodian Government broadcast an appeal for help to the United States and other nations of the free world, stating that it was being invaded by North Vietnamese forces, who had already taken three of its seventeen provinces—five others were in grave danger of falling under their control.

For the US Government, Sihanouk's fall from power and his replacement by an anti-Communist regime presented an ideal opportunity to further secure the South Vietnamese Government against Communist attacks in the face of increased withdrawal of American troops from Southeast Asia. In fact, failure to take this opportunity to strike a death blow against the vast Communist network of support bases in Cambodia might well force a change in the whole American strategy of the war. In addition, a swift strike to destroy Communist logistical facilities by a joint US-South Vietnamese force might provide an ideal test of Vietnamization, reassuring both allies that the passing of combat responsibility was progressing well. The American political aspects of such an operation were fraught with danger, however, and any such decision could come only from the White House.

In early April, such possibilities were discussed by General Abrams, then the Senior US Commander in South Vietnam, and General Cao Van Vien, his South Vietnamese counterpart. They, in turn, dealt through channels with President Thieu, President Nixon and their advisers. It was finally decided to launch a major series of co-ordinated attacks by South Vietnamese and American forces. The targets were to be Communist base camps and logistical installations just across the border in Cambodia.

The massive assault was to take place on 30 April, but a number of smaller raids were carried out before then by South

Vietnamese troops. The two most important, Toan Thang 41 and Cuu Long/SD9/06, were multi-battalion operations carried out on 14 and 20 April as a result of direct orders from President Thieu to South Vietnamese Corps Commanders. Both were bold strikes by infantry-armor task forces (without their US Advisors, who stayed behind in South Vietnam) that met little resistance during the three days each operation required. Major supply caches were captured and destroyed or returned to South Vietnam, but Communist troops were unwilling to stand and fight: they melted away at the first burst of gunfire, leaving massive spoils behind them.

Meanwhile, feverish planning in US and South Vietnamese headquarters was producing the operations plan for a major set of attacks across the Cambodian border at many points. Code names for the incursions were: Toan Thang (Total Victory) for operations conducted by III Corps and the US II Field Force: Cuu Long (Mekong) for operations conducted by IV Corps and the US Delta Military Assistance Command; and Binh Tay (Tame the West) for operations conducted by II Corps and the US I Field Force. The Cambodia-South Vietnam border ran for more than 600 kilometers, from the South China Sea to the three-border area where Laos began, much of it through heavily jungled mountainous areas that seemed forbidding to all transportation but helicopters. The allied incursion was massive, and will be described largely from the perspective of the II, III and IV Corps South Vietnamese Military areas and the troops from each region as they participated.

There were two Communist base areas of particular interest, however, and they were in relatively open country. The first of these was known as the Fishhook, an area some 80 kilometers from Saigon dotted with Communist base camps and supply points; the Central Office South Vietnam (COSVN) was believed to be here. This was the nerve center from which the North Vietnamese command ran the entire war in South Vietnam. The other area was known as the 'Parrot's Beak,' a protuberance in the border that came to within 20 kilometers of Saigon and was also filled with enemy base camps, hospitals and other logistical facilities. These two areas were to be hit by the best American and South Vietnamese troops available, including the US 1st Cavalry Division, 25th Infantry Division and 11th Armored Cavalry Regiment, and South Vietnamese Airborne, Ranger and Armored units. It was expected to take at least a month to clean these areas out, and the weather forecast for May and June indicated that maximum air transportation and tactical air support could be freely used. Attacks were launched in these areas beginning on 29 April 1970: between 30 April and 30 June, massive attacks were launched into Cambodia by South Vietnamese and American forces along the whole length of the border. As part of the original plan, it was agreed that American troops would go no farther than 30km into Cambodia, while South Vietnamese troops would generally restrict themselves to a region within 60km of the border, although a few exceptions would be made to this rule.

In the United States, on the evening of 30 April 1970, President Nixon publicly announced that US and South Vietnamese forces were even then launching attacks into Cambodia. Enormous domestic hostility was anticipated, and did occur, from those Americans opposed to the war in Vietnam. The limited geographical and durational nature of the attacks, however, mitigated some of the opposition expressed. Still, both the general American and South Vietnamese public, as well as their Communist adversaries in Cambodia, were on notice that US forces would be withdrawn from Cambodia by or before 30 June.

On 30 April, the US 1st Cavalry Division (Airmobile) and the South Vietnamese Airborne Division launched a joint attack (Toan Thang 43) into the Fishhook region of Cambodia, with the mission to find and destroy the COSVN headquarters suspected to be located in that region. The border in this region forms a rough right angle, with South Vietnam south and east of the targeted region. In the last few days of April, US and South Vietnamese forces were moved close to the border in anticipation of the co-ordinated attack. The operations plan called for massive air and artillery strikes, followed by heliborne assaults into landing zones north of the area where COSVN headquarters was suspected to be.

The 3rd Brigade of the ARVN Airborne Division would make these assaults and block Communist escape routes to the North. Meanwhile, the 3rd Brigade of the 1st Cavalry Division and the tanks and armored personnel carriers of the 11th Armored Cavalry Regiment, would be attacking from the south and southwest. The 1st Battalion, 9th Infantry, 1st Cavalry Division, would be conducting reconnaissance patrols by helicopter and on the ground to the north of the ARVN Airborne Division. Other units would step up operations in South Vietnam to the east of the objective area, to preclude Communist evasion in that direction.

Just before midnight on 30 April, and through the early morning hours of 1 May, massive air attacks pummeled the target area, including many B-52 strikes. By daylight, the bombing was replaced by concentrated artillery barrages, in both the suspected COSVN location and the area where ARVN airborne troops would be landed in the north. Landing zones were cleared in the thick jungles by dropping enormous 15,000-lb bombs followed by tactical air strikes and artillery barrages. By 8:00 in the morning the ARVN airborne units were arriving on the newly cleared landing zones, and meeting surprisingly little or no opposition. From the air, however, Communist forces were caught scrambling. The 1st of the 9th, patrolling to the north, observed and fired upon many Communists' trucks and other vehicles fleeing the area. While the ARVN airborne had met little resistance as they arrived, this changed as they moved south on the ground. However, the Communists refused to tie into any set-piece battles, a situation also discovered by forces attacking from the south. But massive Communist stocks of logistical supplies were being discovered along with large supporting installations.

Prisoners captured in the early stages of the operation were from the 250th Rehabilitation Unit, the 50th Rear Security Unit and the 165th Regiment, 7th North Vietnamese Division. Medical supplies, hospitals, truck parts, vehicle-service facilities, massive weapons and ammunition caches were being discovered every day, readily abandoned by Communist forces, who seemed to prefer losing materiel to fighting. Given the well-advertised 60-day nature of this incursion, however, its limited geographical extent, and the virtually helpless nature of the Cambodian national forces supposedly opposed to Communist troops throughout the rest of Cambodia, this decision to avoid combat was probably a wise Communist move. The main American goal seemed to be to buy time by destroying Communist supply depots and logistical facilities, while at the same time promoting major semi-independent combat operations by large South Vietnamese units. The Communists expected that they would be able to return to their border sanctuaries after the 60-day operation, although they would have to do considerable rebuilding and refurbishing. While the South Vietnamese would still be able to operate across the Cambodian border after the 60-day period, their American Advisors would not be able to accompany them, and it was unclear just how effective they would be in that mode.

On 3 May the 2nd Brigade of the US 1st Cavalry Division arrived to support the operation in the Fishhook region. Aerial observation had discovered sizable enemy installations in the jungle to the northwest of this area, where COSVN was believed to be located. Infantry troops were guided into the area, and so many buildings and caches were discovered that US forces named it 'The City.' An extensive search of the area, some three square kilometers in size, was made from 5 to 13 May. Among the discoveries were hundreds of buildings including 18 messhalls, two hospitals well supplied with medicine and equipment, a large training base, a farm with hundreds of chickens and pigs, over 300 vehicles, thousands of individual and crew-served weapons, hundreds of tons of ammunition, thousands of uniforms and thousands of tons of foodstuffs. Although no documents were found identifying this as COSVN headquarters, and no prisoners admitted to any association with COSVN, this was clearly a major logistical base for Communist forces.

The first attacks, as mentioned earlier, had been launched into the Angel's Wing area of the Parrot's Beak on 14 April and then farther to the south and west on 20 April. The major combined incursion to follow did not see US troops cross the Cambodian border until 30 April, but the first attacks of this operation occurred on 29 April by three multi-battalion ARVN infantry—armored task forces from III Corps—denominated 318, 333 and 225—in Operation Toan Thang 42. They crossed the border into the Parrot's Beak on the morning of the 29th, lunging deep into Cambodia. Initial resistance was light, but stiffened on the 30th when strongly fortified Communist positions were encountered. The armored forces were hesitant, during the first few days, to attack once contact was made, but the Ranger and Infantry battalions attached to each task force were able to take all objectives without tank support. Within a few days, commanders were able to pressure the armored units into leading assaults or moving to the attack accompanied by foot-soldiers, according to more conventional tactics. The joint armor-infantry attacks, thereafter, were rarely even slowed.

On 2 May Task Forces 333 and 225 turned and attacked to the south of Route 1, while 318 continued west on Route 1. That day, on the southern side of the Parrot's Beak, IV Corps units consisting of the ARVN 9th Infantry Division, five armored cavalry squadrons and four ranger battalions attacked to the north. By this time, fighting raged along most of the border, as US and ARVN rolled, flew, or walked into Cambodia. These combined III Corps—IV Corps forces occupied the Parrot's Beak until 5 May, destroying Communist defensive positions with air support, artillery, armor and infantry attacks. During that time, 1010 Communist soldiers, mostly from the North Vietnamese 9th Division, were killed and 204 captured; over 1000 individual and crew-served weapons were taken, and over 100 tons of assorted ammunition were destroyed.

On 5 May IV Corps forces were withdrawn from the Parrot's Beak and prepared to move to the south and west and stage another border crossing up the Mekong River with a major US and South Vietnamese naval force. The III Corps forces in the Parrot's Beak moved west on Route 1, clearing and holding Cambodian territory as they moved.

On 9 May the ARVN 9th Infantry Division, 21st Infantry Division, five armored cavalry squadrons, a marine brigade and about 100 South Vietnamese and US Navy ships crossed the border and moved up the Mekong River toward Pnom Penh in Operation Cuu Long. Their mission was to clear the Mekong, but also to rescue tens of thousands of South Vietnamese civilians being detained in camps in Pnom Penh and Kompong Cham—clearly an uncomfortable reappearance of ethnic rivalry among supposed allies fighting Communism. The US Cougar Task Force helicopters carried many infantrymen to Neak Luong, a town some two-thirds of the distance to Pnom Penh, beyond which US personnel would not proceed. On 11 May the naval task force and the armor-infantry forces clearing both banks of the Mekong arrived in Neak Luong, as did the 318 Task Force from III Corps, which had cleared Route 1 and moved up from the South Vietnamese border.

American ships remained in Neak Luong, and South Vietnamese forces continued on to Pnom Penh, which they reached that day. On 12 May they proceeded to Kompong Cham. Some 9000 Vietnamese refugees were picked up there and returned to Pnom Penh, where an additional 8000 Vietnamese boarded the ships. The entire flotilla, with 17,000 added passengers, crossed back into South Vietnam on 13 May. During the period of incursion, the South Vietnamese left three marine battalions and two river groups at Neak Luong, which thereafter served as a key logistical support base for South Vietnamese forces in Cambodia.

On 6 May Toan Thang 44 was launched by the US 25th Infantry Division, with the objective of destroying Communist Base Area 354 in Cambodia west of Tay Ninh Province. Division engineers had to construct a pontoon bridge across the Ben Go River for armored vehicles, but this was quickly done; on 7 May armored infantry units attacked west and south. Many heavy engagements occurred, but, as elsewhere, Communist troops refused to be pinned down, especially by the heavy weaponry and armament of these American troops. Huge supply caches were uncovered, but on 14 May the operation ended, and units of the 25th Infantry Division were transported to the Fishhook region to relieve the US 1st Air Cavalry Division.

On 6 May Toan Thang 45 was also launched by the 2nd

Brigade, US 1st Cavalry Division against Communist Base Area 351 in Cambodia. Two battalions made a heliborne combat assault into the area that day, and met only light resistance. The next day, however, they discovered an enemy weapons-and-ammunition cache so large that it was decided to build a road out to transport the captured munitions, since it would have taken many days of valuable helicopter time to accomplish the task. The spoils were so rich in this area that by 20 May, eight full battalions had been deployed to engage in the search. During the second week in June, an underground communications depot was discovered that, according to captured documents, belonged to COSVN headquarters. On 20 June the 1st Cavalry began dismantling its fire bases and returning to South Vietnam. By 27 June the 1st Cavalry Division had left Cambodia, and Communist Base Area 351 was pulverized thereafter by massive B-52 strikes.

Also on 6 May Toan Thang 46 was launched by the 9th Regiment, ARVN 5th Infantry Division against Communist base Area 350 in Cambodia. They were transported into the area by American helicopters, and initial opposition was light, but the quantities of munitions and equipment found were startling. Communist opposition began to intensify, and on 11 May the ARVN 1st Armored Cavalry Squadron came in as reinforcements. A major battle erupted on 21 May, but with effective air and artillery support, the ARVN soon routed the Communists. Then they discovered what had been worth extraordinary Communist protection—a 500-bed hospital, with modern surgical facilities and plentiful medicine and equipment, and a major truck park and repair facility. The discoveries that followed through June were smaller, but in the aggregate it was clear that the Communists had paid a heavy logistical price. By 27 June the ARVN units from Toan Thang 46 were back on their side of the border.

Meanwhile, up north in II Corps, major ARVN and US forces moved into the heavily jungled mountainous area of Cambodia directly to their west in Operation Binh Tay. The principal forces in this action were the ARVN 22nd and 23rd Infantry Division, the 2nd Ranger Group and the 2nd Armor Brigade; US forces were drawn from the 4th Infantry Division. The objective of this operation was to attack and destroy Communist Base Area 702, a massive logistical support area covering a wide region of Cambodia west of Pleiku.

On 6 and 7 May the 1st Brigade of the US 4th Infantry Division was inserted into the objective area. Although the countryside had been struck with heavy artillery fire and air strikes before the helicopter troop transports arrived, the Communist anti-aircraft fire from the ground was still quite heavy and kept some battalions from landing. By 7 May, however, the entire 1st Brigade was on the ground and heavily engaged with enemy forces. When the 2nd Brigade arrived later in the day, resistance slackened. The discoveries of Communist supplies and logistical facilities were massive, but after 7 May, little contact was sustained with Communist forces. By 15 May these two American Brigades had been replaced by the ARVN 22nd Infantry Division and the 2nd Ranger Group. Major discoveries continued until 25 May, when the operation ended.

On 14 May Operation Binh Tay II was launched by the ARVN 22nd Infantry Division and the 2nd Armored Brigade, against Base Area 701. For two weeks these units moved freely through the objective area, discovering additional Communist caches and logistical facilities, but making only rare contact with the enemy. On 27 May the ARVN units had returned to South Vietnam. Operation Binh Tay III followed from 20 May to 27 June, conducted by the ARVN 23rd Infantry Division against Communist Base Area 740 in Cambodia. As with Binh Tay II, contacts with Communist forces were scattered and never serious, but the discoveries of munitions and logistical facilities were dramatic.

By 30 June, as promised, all US military forces had left Cambodia. South Vietnamese forces had made no such promises, and they made a number of later incursions. The final tally for this two-month effort showed 11,369 Communists killed and 2328 taken prisoner (roughly the fighting strength of an entire division). Some 538 South Vietnamese and 338 Americans lost their lives, and 3009 South Vietnamese and 1525 Americans were wounded. Over 25,000 weapons were captured, along with 435 vehicles, millions of small-arms rounds, hundreds of thousands of mortar rounds and rockets, tons of pharmaceutical and food supplies.

Over a short term, the Cambodian incursion was of considerable benefit to both the United States and South Vietnam. The destruction of the Communist bases largely eliminated the immediate logistical support mechanisms through which North Vietnam supported their war with South Vietnam. However, by usually avoiding prolonged contact, the Communists were able to keep major forces largely intact within Cambodia (the Cambodian military provided no real obstacle to the Communists). They knew (like the rest of the world) that the American incursion would last only 60 days, and, in the long run, they could afford to lose the stores and installations they had to abandon.

This operation gave the South Vietnamese military their first real chance to conduct large conventional operations semi-independently, and the success they realized in this no doubt built up their confidence and their esprit de corps; for the first time, they believed that perhaps they could fight and win without Americans fighting for them. The Communists were forced, very slowly and tediously, to build up their logistical infrastructure all over again. It took years to do, but time, as it turned out, was on their side.

LUNGE INTO LAOS

LAOS

Lam Son 719

Prior to 1970 massive resupplies and reinforcements were sent from North Vietnam to the Communist troops in South Vietnam via two primary routes. The first of these was the Ho Chi Minh Trail. The other route was by cargo ship into the Cambodian port of Sihanoukville, then across Cambodia and into South Vietnam. Given the distances involved, this was a much faster and more efficient way to resupply Communist troops in the southern half of South Vietnam. Prince Sihanouk, the Cambodian ruler, had long allowed the North Vietnamese and their allies to use this major port and his territory for trans-shipment of supplies and reinforcements, and even for construction of major base areas and logistical facilities.

But in March 1970 Prince Sihanouk was over thrown and replaced by an anti-Communist government that ordered North Vietnamese forces out of Cambodia and invited US and South Vietnamese forces to clean out the Communist sanctuaries just inside the border. This they did during May and June 1970, capturing or destroying a true mountain of supplies and support equipment. When they returned to South Vietnam, Communist forces were able to return to and re-establish administrative centers and logistical facilities, but they had enormous rebuilding and refurbishing duties before them to make these base areas operational again. But with

Sihanouk's fall the Communists had lost the use of the port of Sihanoukville—renamed Kompong Som by his successors. Now all supplies and reinforcements had to make the long, arduous and dangerous trip down the Ho Chi Minh Trail, subject to continual threat of bombing by US planes.

This caused a dramatic increase in traffic on the Ho Chi Minh Trail, as the North Vietnamese scrambled to re-establish their base camp system in Cambodia. The South Vietnamese and American military were eager to follow their successful Cambodian incursion with another deep, telling blow. An invasion of Laos near the DMZ became an attractive idea; it would be another bold stroke by South Vietnam (now on the offensive for the first time), it would interrupt the flow of reinforcements and supplies to South Vietnam and it might make North Vietnam dramatically alter its strategy.

By 1970 the Ho Chi Minh Trail had been developed into an elaborate system of some 3600 kilometers of roads and trails running south down a wide corridor. It was maintained by North Vietnamese troops in Transportation Group 559 and civilian workers, numbering around 150,000. They were equipped with plentiful anti-aircraft weapons of all sorts, but their primary duties turned on operation and maintenance of the trail: engineering, transportation, storage, service, medical support. Trucks carried only supplies and heavy weapons or equipment; lighter equipment was carried by individuals or animals. Troop reinforcements marched on trails different from those used by trucks. They usually moved in battalion strength of 500 to 600 men, and it could take 100 days or more to reach their destinations in South Vietnam. By 1970 Group 559 had established many 'Binh Trams' (troop stations) a day's march apart, where trucks and troops could find shelter and sustenance, as well as other logistical support. Each Binh Tram was responsible for a specific area of the trail and was a self-contained logistical organization, including an assigned regiment of infantry and anti-aircraft troops.

In early January 1971, General Abrams, Commanding General of US Forces in Vietnam, proposed to General Vien, the South Vietnamese Minister of Defense, that the South Vietnamese launch an attack into Laos from the vicinity of

Khe Sanh on Route 9. South Vietnamese forces were eager for such an operation, and President Thieu quickly approved it, whereupon US and South Vietnamese commanders and staff officers speedily worked out the details. The operation was to be known as Lam Son 719, to be carried out in four phases, with the objectives of cutting the diverse lines of the Ho Chi Minh Trail that flowed through the area, and destroying enemy forces and facilities, in particular Communist Base Areas 604 and 611. It was to be launched on 1 February, and was to extend over an indefinite period, although all indications showed that it was to last some 90 days, or until the rainy season arrived in Laos in early May. No US ground forces or advisers would enter Laos, but this timetable would allow optimal use of US air support, both for transportation and as a tactical weapon.

Four phases were proposed for the operation. The first would consist of US units reopening the Khe Sanh base, clearing Route 9 up to the Laotian border and assembling massive artillery and air-support forces. Phase II would be an ARVN infantry-armor attack down Route 9 into Laos, with co-ordinated advance attacks on neighboring high ground where fire-support bases (FSBs) would be established. Phase II would continue until the major trail intersection in the town of Tchepone, some 40 kilometers west of the South Vietnamese border, was taken. Phase III would be the exploitation phase, when search operations would fan out from Tchepone to destroy enemy forces and bases, and disrupt traffic on the Ho Chi Minh Trail. Phase IV would be the orderly withdrawal of South Vietnamese troops from Laos.

Enemy forces in the objective area were suspected to include three regular infantry regiments as well as three or four Binh Trams of regiment size. It was estimated that within two weeks, up to eight more infantry regiments could arrive from North Vietnam, along with artillery, engineers and other support troops. Only eight South Vietnamese infantry regiments or brigades and one armored brigade of tanks were originally to be committed to this operation, but the Binh Trams were not believed to be manned by troops prepared for sustained ground combat operations. The planners also believed that a strike by tank-supported troops down Route 9, with the assistance of fire-support bases established on high ground flanking both sides of the road, would be fast and effective, and that Tchepone and the major intersection of the Ho Chi Minh Trail there would fall before the North Vietnamese could react. Thereafter, spoiling raids into the massive storage areas known to surround Tchepone would keep the Communists on the defensive, forcing them to react to unpredictable South Vietnamese attacks. With the promise of massive air support ranging from B-52 raids to helicopter gunships and troop transports, South Vietnamese commanders felt they were poised to strike effectively. The troops to be used on this operation—the Airborne Division, the Marine Division, the 1st Ranger Group, the 1st Infantry Division and the 1st Armor Brigade—were elite units, with the highest reputations for courage and fighting ability. But the execution by their commanders was to drag, which forced an early and hurried end to the operation, thus defeating many high expectations.

The first phase was launched on 30 January, when the 1st Brigade of the US 4th Infantry Division landed by helicopter in the Khe Sanh area, quickly securing the abandoned US Marine Base there with little opposition. On 1 February US heavy artillery units arrived at Khe Sanh and dug their guns into position while an engineering battalion began to repair the airstrip. On 3 February the 1st Ranger Group arrived in the Phu Loc area northwest of Khe Sanh, where they established an FSB. On 4 through 6 February, elements of the ARVN Airborne Division, the 1st Armor Brigade, and the 1st Infantry Division began to assemble in the Khe Sanh area. By 7 February all ARVN assault forces and US support units were in position and ready to go. US support included the helicopter assets of the 101st Airborne Division plus helicopters from many other units that had been attached to the 101st for this operation; eight 8-inch guns and twenty 175mm guns represented the heaviest artillery pieces in the US arsenal.

Phase II was launched on 8 February. Eleven B-52 strikes went into Laos just before dawn, concentrating on suspected

Communist positions as well as anticipated helicopter landing zones. At seven in the morning the first airborne-armor task force crossed the border and began moving into Laos on Route 9. It consisted of two tank squadrons from the 1st Armor Brigade, two battalions of infantry from the Airborne Division and a combat engineer battalion complete with a platoon of bulldozers to effect repairs to the road surface. They were covered by a flight of US helicopter gunships, who struck at Communist positions in the hills on both sides of the road. While no American troops, whether units or advisers, would be present on the ground with the ARVN forces, the whole operation was strongly dependent on US helicopter and fighter-bomber support, which would play a crucial role as events unfolded.

As the airborne-armor force moved down Route 9, the supporting assault units made helicopter landings on the hill-tops where they proposed to establish their first FSBs. Units of the 1st Infantry Division landed at Landing Zones (LZs) Hotel and Blue without Communist opposition. Battalions from the 3rd Brigade of the Airborne Division had similar free rides as they took LZs 30 and 31. The arrival of the 21st Ranger Battalion at LZ Ranger South, however, was met with Communist anti-aircraft machine-gun fire. US gunship support was needed before they could overrun the high ground and begin to establish the defenses of an FSB. By nightfall the armored column had moved only nine kilometers into Laos because of bad road conditions. During the night, US gunships attacked trucks near Ban Dong, the first objective on Route 9 on the way to Tchepone. On 9 February heavy rain flooded the road, and the armored column did not move at all. A battalion from the 1st Infantry Division went into LZ Delta. Air strikes again lit up the otherwise dreary night.

On 10 February the weather cleared a little, and the armored column picked up speed. At 5:00 PM, the 9th Airborne Battalion arrived at Ban Dong through a hail of anti-aircraft fire and drove off the Communists they found on the ground. Two hours later, the armored column began to arrive via Route 9. A number of helicopters had been shot down that day, however, and Communist resistance began to stiffen.

Artillery batteries were placed on FSBs 30, 31, Ban Dong, Hotel and Delta. The 39th Ranger Battalion went into LZ Ranger North.

From 11 to 16 February the armored column did not proceed beyond Ban Dong. This was the first action—or inaction—that indicated a lack of the resolve necessary to carry off a sudden strike deep into the heart of enemy territory. While the more audacious commanders, supported by the Americans, pressured to continue the attack, South Vietnamese political and military leadership in Saigon vacillated. Each hour of indecision turned to the advantage of the North Vietnamese, who were moving troops down from North Vietnam.

During this week of indecision the Rangers to the north were in daily contact with varying Communist forces. Other ARVN units searched the areas around their FSBs, but most of the Communist bodies and equipment recovered were the result of B-52 and other air strikes. As events were to show, this was truly the lull before the storm.

During this period of inactivity on Route 9, the 1st Infantry Division had been expanding steadily to the south and west, placing battalions at LZs Delta 1, Grass and Don. These battalions began patrolling aggressively, engaging in prolonged firefights with Communist forces and discovering large base areas and supply caches. To their north, the Rangers and Airborne were meeting growing opposition around their FSBs, but the armored column did not move. Finally, on 16 February, the order came to continue the armored movement to the west, establishing FSBs in the hills on either side of Route 9 as planned, and to get to Tchepone as quickly as possible.

On 17 February heavy rain precluded most helicopter support and cover, but north of Ban Dong a Communist PT-76 tank was captured, and there were indications that a number of fresh North Vietnamese divisions had recently arrived in the area. On 18 and 19 February the 102nd Regiment of the 308th North Vietnamese Division began attacking the 39th and 21st Ranger battalions at FSBs Ranger North and South. On 19 February the South Vietnamese Government and military leaders in Saigon once again became hesitant, and delayed any further movement west by the armored column until matters were cleared up in the Ranger area. During the night, heavy US air and artillery strikes were placed around both Ranger positions. It now appeared that the 64th Regiment of the North Vietnamese 320th Division was also involved in the attack.

During the day on 20 February Communist anti-aircraft fire around the Ranger FSBs was intense, and helicopter support was next to impossible. That afternoon, a helicopter pilot reported seeing 400 to 500 Communist troops encircling Ranger North, where the 39th Ranger Battalion was located. Just before dark, Communist forces overran the defenses. Within a few hours, 199 survivors from the 39th who managed to fall back before the Communist attack reached Ranger South and the 21st Ranger battalion. Another 330 members of the 39th were dead or captured. Although it was believed that Communist forces attacking Ranger North had suffered even larger casualties as a result of the withering artillery and air support, the mood was somber that night at Ranger South.

On 22 February a massive air and artillery strike around Ranger South allowed medical evacuation helicopters to extract 122 wounded Rangers. The Operation Commander decided that Ranger South was draining too much air and artillery support, and was not necessary to the move west toward Tchepone. On 24 February he decided to close it, and that day extracted the 500 Rangers remaining there from the 21st and 39th Battalions and returned them to South Vietnam.

In the south two battalions of the 1st Infantry Division were engaged in heavy combat with Communist forces on 23 February. During the early hours of 24 February, two battalions were pulled back and a B-52 strike hit Communist positions. The two battalions returned to the attack with dawn, finding 159 Communist bodies and weapons as well as numerous blood trails. But strong Communist forces continued to squeeze FSB Hotel II, which delayed movement of 1st Infantry Division elements to the west.

With the withdrawal of Ranger battalions from Ranger North and South, the Airborne Division units at FSBs 30 and 31 became the main target of Communist attacks from the north. The North Vietnamese 304th, 308th and 320th Divisions as well as several artillery regiments, an armored regiment and three air defense regiments, had been sent into the area since 8 February to stop Lam Son 719. FSBs 30 and 31 were each defended by an Airborne battalion. On the night of 23 February, heavy Communist mortar fire hit FSB 31, where the headquarters of the 3rd Brigade, Airborne Division was also located. The defenses were probed by small-arms and mortar fire for the next 24 hours. On the morning of 25 February, the incoming fire was greatly increased by a number of Communist 130mm field guns, and counterbattery fire was called in from FSBs 30 and Ban Dong, as well as the 105mm battery on FSB 31. Just after noon, enemy armored movements were detected to the south. By two o'clock, enemy tanks had reached the wire at the southern perimeter of the base. Fighter-bombers stopped this attack by destroying a number of tanks just as they breached the defenses of FSB 31. Shortly after three o'clock, however, some 20 tanks and waves of supporting Communist infantry attacked from the northwest and east at the same time. By four o'clock, FSB 31 had been overwhelmed. Many paratroopers managed to break out and avoid capture, but 155 were killed or captured in that final assault, including the commander of the 3rd Brigade of the Airborne Division.

In the next five days, an armored-infantry task force consisting of one squadron of tanks and one battalion of paratroopers fought three battles to reach the site of FSB 31 and rescue those soldiers who had evaded the Communist forces. The ARVN lost 28 tanks and other armored vehicles, while the Communists lost 23. Tanks had suddenly assumed unexpected importance in the heavily overgrown mountainous terrain.

The Communists began to apply pressure on FSB 30 and other FSBs south of Route 9. Anti-aircraft fire was becoming intense, bringing down helicopters like flies. Many FSBs were effectively shut off from resupply or medical evacuation, and major artillery preparations had to be laid down before the high-risk helicopter runs could even be attempted. After two helicopters were blown out of the air attempting to extract artillery pieces from FSB Hotel II, it was decided to destroy the artillery pieces on the ground and have the 3rd Regiment of the 1st Infantry Division move on foot to the northwest. B-52 strikes were slaughtering Communist troops continually, but they seemed to pour into the area in an unending stream. Once again, the move west by the armored column was stalled.

In Saigon, President Thieu and his military leaders decided to reinforce Lam Son 719 with the Marine Division. The three regiments of the 1st Infantry Division, who had fared better against the enemy than the other troops on this operation, would be helilifted into the Tchepone area, while the Marine Division replaced them south of Route 9. The Airborne Division and the armored Brigade were basically directed to hold their ground on Route 9 and north of it. It had become obvious that, because of indecision in the South Vietnamese command structure, there was little likelihood the armored column would ever reach Tchepone: that likelihood lessened each day as more Communist troops arrived from North Vietnam to preclude it. It was obvious that the most face-saving way of extracting themselves from a tight position would be insertion of token units into Tchepone, where they would show the flag, and then quickly pull all forces back into the relative safety of South Vietnam.

From the time FSB 31 fell on 25 February until 3 March, FSB 30 had been subject to a continual artillery barrage; twice armor-infantry attacks by Communist forces were turned back only by timely air support. By 3 March, however, none of the 12 artillery pieces on FSB 30 was functioning. It was decided to abandon FSB 30, and after destroying their artillery pieces and evacuating their wounded by helicopter, the battalion of paratroopers moved back toward Route 9 on the ground.

On 2 March the Marine Brigades began to arrive at FSBs Delta and Hotel, relieving troops from the 1st Infantry Division to close on Tchepone. On 3 March a battalion of the 1st Infantry landed at LZ Lolo in the face of fierce ground fire, which shot down 11 helicopters. On 4 March another battalion landed at Lolo, where bulldozers quickly built an

FSB, and a third landed at LZ Liz nearby, where the same entrenchment took place. (The Western names for LZs and FSBs may seem strange for a South Vietnamese operation, but they were chosen by South Vietnamese commanders to ensure that American pilots and artillery personnel would be dealing with names they could understand and pronounce.)

On 5 March the entire 2nd Regiment—three battalions—of the 1st Infantry Division landed at LZ Sophia; by nightfall, eight artillery pieces were well dug in there. During the afternoon, two battalions had patrolled the surrounding area and discovered hundreds of bodies of Communist soldiers recently killed by B-52 strikes. From FSB Sophia, Tchepone was within easy reach of these elements of the 1st Infantry Division.

On 6 March 120 US helicopters had been prepared to carry out the assault on LZ Hope, which was preceded by major B-52 strikes in the Tchepone area. Two battalions of the 1st Infantry Division landed at Hope that afternoon. As they patrolled south, hundreds of North Vietnamese bodies were reported in the aftermath of the massive air strikes that day. Next day Communist gunners found the range of FSB Lolo, which was soon in a state of siege. Elements of the 2nd Regiment, 1st ARVN Infantry Division claim to have darted briefly into Tchepone and then quickly withdrawn (a claim later disputed by the North Vietnamese, who insist the South Vietnamese never reached Tchepone). Whatever the case, the town of Tchepone had been bombed back to the Stone Age, but the original ARVN plan of using it as a base for spoiling raids into North Vietnamese storage facilities and base areas was not to be realized. In fact, having claimed at least to have touched their symbolic goal, the South Vietnamese forces quickly set about trying to effect an orderly withdrawal. But with the Communist pressure growing on their flanks, the withdrawal of some South Vietnamese units became a rush for survival. As ARVN forces turned back toward their border, the tables were turned on them; they were defending themselves as they tried to execute what was basically an orderly retreat under fire, the most difficult of all military movements.

On 10 March the 2nd Regiment of the 1st Infantry Division began to move from FSB Sophia to FSB Liz; from there they were helilifted to FSB Sophia East. The 1st Regiment was searching the Ta Luong area and moving down Route 914, where enormous damage to Communist base areas from B-52 strikes was discovered. On 12 March the last ARVN troops were lifted out of FSBs Liz and Sophia, and US tactical air strikes destroyed the artillery pieces they had been forced to abandon.

On 13 March FSB Lolo began to receive such intensive artillery fire that no helicopters could land there. The 1st Regiment was now operating in Gia Lam and Back Mai areas, finding treasure troves of Communist supplies. However, they were ordered to move east, and the units in the FSB Lolo area broke through the Communist cordon on 15 March, lunging toward Route 9. One battalion held out at Lolo until the 16th, when it, too, tried desperately to reach Route 9 and helicopter extraction. Only 32 survivors made it, leaving behind hundreds of their brothers, either dead or in Communist hands.

On 19 March, the armored column abandoned Ban Dong and moved east to a position near FSB Alpha. The Marines at FSBs south of Route 9 were now subject to heavy Communist assaults and were fighting hard to stay afloat. The 324th North Vietnamese Division had just arrived in the area and was making a special effort to destroy the Marine bases. On 20 March, an 18-vehicle convoy from Ban Dong—the last in line—was ambushed on Route 9 and destroyed. Now terror began to overtake some of the South Vietnamese soldiers.

On 21 March the last elements of the 1st Infantry Division were helilifted back into South Vietnam. The 29th and 803rd Regiments of the 324B NVA Division made an all-out effort to destroy FSB Delta, held by a Marine brigade. Their human-wave attacks with tanks were repulsed four times with massive air attacks and a B-52 mission in late afternoon. The Marines lost 85 killed and 238 wounded that day, but counted over 600 Communist bodies outside their defenses the next morning. Also on the 21st, an armored squadron and an airborne battalion were heavily engaged on Route 9 near FSB Bravo. These ARVN forces lost nearly a hundred men before nightfall, and 17 tanks and armored vehicles.

US air strikes were stepped up during this period, as well as major artillery barrages from American batteries just across the border in South Vietnam. But Communist tanks were now appearing in the jungle in hot pursuit of the withdrawing South Vietnamese forces. Panic began to set in, and some South Vietnamese troops lost their heads, giving rise to distressing news clips that showed South Vietnamese soldiers clinging to the skids of Huey helicopters as they arrived in South Vietnam from Laos. Commanders did what they could to maintain order in their units, but in some instances fear surged through the men like riptide, causing them to race for the border at all costs.

On 22 March the Marines were driven off FSB Delta by flame-throwing Communist tanks, and began streaming through the jungle toward FSB Hotel. On 23 March the Marines were evacuated back to South Vietnam by helicopter. Air and military strikes were slowing Communist forces, but a major South Vietnamese effort was being made to prevent an all-out rout. Around noon on 23 March, the last vehicles of the armored column crossed into South Vietnam. On 24 March the last elements of the Marine Division and the Airborne Division were extracted by helicopter. Lam Son 719 ended with dozens of Communist tanks lined up on the border and firing after the retreating South Vietnamese troops.

The after-action report showed that 102 Americans (mostly air crews) were killed in the operation, 215 were wounded and 53 were missing. The South Vietnamese reported losses of 1146 killed, 4236 wounded and 246 missing. Some 92 American and South Vietnamese helicopters had been destroyed, five fixed-wing aircraft, 71 tanks, 96 artillery pieces and 278 trucks. Estimates of Communist losses were around 13,000 killed and 100 tanks and 290 trucks destroyed.

The operation was well launched, and the initial successes should have been followed up forcefully. But once Ban Dong was reached, indecision and hesitation began to set in at command levels. The brief presence of South Vietnamese troops in Tchepone was only for show, and the operation had already been sapped of its vigor on Route 9. Had it not been for massive US air and artillery support, an operation with mixed results might have been turned into a disastrous rout.

THE EASTER
OFFENSIVE OF
1972

After Lam Son 719, South Vietnamese military leaders were appropriately chastened: they redoubled their efforts to train and equip their expanded military to replace the US units leaving Southeast Asia at an accelerated rate. The handwriting was on the wall: the general American public seemed to have turned against the war in Vietnam, and President Nixon's promise of 'Peace with Honor' seemed only a thinly veiled rationale for the extrication of US forces and funds from what seemed a no-win enterprise. As American forces withdrew, combat assets provided to South Vietnamese forces were also reduced, even as the threat from North Vietnam seemed to become more ominous.

It was widely expected that North Vietnam would launch an all-out offensive against South Vietnam as soon as the Americans had withdrawn. Their self-confidence had been boosted by the outcome of Lam Son 719, where they drove the elite of South Vietnamese forces from Laos in disarray, and were stopped only by massive US air and artillery support. Most observers were sure they would wait for their final onslaught until the Americans had left, but for the North Vietnamese, it was a close call. By January 1972, US forces in Vietnam would number only 140,000; by April, that number would be down to 70,000. If the North Vietnamese allowed another year of pacification and Vietnamization to take

place, it might help. Besides, if they were able to conquer
South Vietnam while the Americans were still there in force,
that would make America the loser as well.

Preparations for a major invasion by North Vietnam were
noted by the South Vietnamese as early as late 1971, with
most intelligence estimates predicting that the Tet lunar holiday at the end of January would be marked again by a major
Communist offensive. South Vietnamese troops were alerted
to this, but the period passed uneventfully. Signs of North
Vietnamese preparations continued to increase, but when the
explosion finally came, it was far beyond most expectations.

It was the end of March 1972 before North Vietnam committed practically its entire combat force, 12 divisions and
many separate regiments (whose armament included some
500 tanks and even more artillery pieces) to a massive conventional invasion of South Vietnam on three fronts. The first
attack was in northernmost I Corps, where four divisions of
the North Vietnamese Army (NVA) attacked across the DMZ,
while two other divisions attacked toward Quang Tri and Hue
out of Laos to the west. The second attack was in the Central
Highlands of II Corps, where two NVA Divisions assaulted
Kontum while a third division attacked in the lowlands near
the coast. The third attack came out of Cambodia into III
Corps, where three NVA Divisions washed south toward
Saigon, but were stopped at An Loc.

The initial months of April and May belonged mostly to
the North Vietnamese invaders, but during June the South
Vietnamese stiffened and began to take the offensive. In July
and August they pushed the Communist invaders back, and
by autumn, most of the territory that had fallen into the
attackers' hands was back under South Vietnamese control.
The major battles that raged during what became known as
the Communist Easter Offensive were fought entirely by
South Vietnamese troops, although American Advisers were
on the ground with them. There is no doubt that the strong
air support and bountiful logistical assistance provided by the
Americans were key to the South Vietnamese victory. Never-
theless, it was *their* victory, the long-awaited battlefield test
of 'Vietnamization' for the entire South Vietnamese military.
Their success here did much to erase the negative image that

had been attached to them by many observers after their hasty termination of the Lam Son 719 foray into Communist-controlled Laos in 1971. We will examine the battles on each of these three fronts in some detail.

Quang Tri City

The 3rd ARVN Division was responsible, in the spring of 1972, for northernmost Quang Tri Province and the Demilitarized Zone (DMZ), a role once filled by the US Marine Corps. The 3rd Division had been activated only in the fall of 1971, and although it had never fought together as a unit, its component battalions were battle-hardened outfits with long experience in the area. To the south of Quang Tri Province, the other I Corps forces were the 1st and 2nd Divisions, the 51st Infantry Regiment, the 51st Ranger Group (of 9 battalions), the 1st Armor Brigade, artillery units and local regional and popular forces. The 1st Division had two South Vietnamese Marine Brigades attached to it, which were established at Fire Support Base (FSB) Nancy and at Mai Loc Combat Base. The 3rd Division Headquarters were at Quang Tri Combat Base, while its units were on a string of FSBs and strong points south of the DMZ and to the west of Dong Ha and Quang Tri City.

The Communist attack came at noon on 30 March, in the form of major artillery barrages against the 3rd ARVN Division positions, followed by strong armor-infantry forces attacking south across the DMZ in four columns. Within a few hours, four more columns came streaming out of the west as artillery fire struck the FSBs in that area. FSBs Sarge and Nui Ba Ho were overrun in the early morning hours of 1 April. By that afternoon, the whole northern string of FSBs had been abandoned, sometimes with still-functioning artillery pieces that could all-too-easily be turned on the retreating ARVN forces. At 6:00 PM the 3rd Division Commander ordered all units north of Dong Ha to withdraw to the southern bank of the Cua Viet River. On the west, Camp Carroll and FSB Mai Loc were still under firm South Vietnamese control.

On 2 April Communist attacks continued. The bridge at

Dong Ha was destroyed before the North Vietnamese troops reached it, but the 56th Regiment—one-third of the strength of the 3rd Division—was surrounded by NVA troops at Camp Carroll, and its commander surrendered at nightfall. When that happened, the Marines at Mai Loc fell back to Quang Tri City, and the noose tightened. The ARVN stiffened thereafter, and the Communists were unable to advance farther for another week. During that time, 12 Ranger Battalions and three Marine Battalions arrived as reinforcements in Quang Tri City.

On 9 April a major attack was launched by the NVA 304th and 308th Divisions and two regiments of tanks, but they were unable to break through ARVN defenses. US tactical air strikes punished Communist ranks, and they withdrew before nightfall. Artillery duels filled the next week and more, and on 19 April a tactical blunder caused the fall of Dong Ha: the 1st Armor Brigade pulled a squadron of tanks from their defensive positions south of the Cua Viet River during a Communist artillery barrage and had them move south on Highway 1 to clear enemy action to the west. Surrounding troops, not knowing why the tanks were moving, assumed the defensive line had been broken and, unwilling to be left behind, streamed in panic after the tank column. By the time cooler heads could prevail, the defensive line had been lost, and a new one had to be formed north of the Thach Han River. This position held for several weeks, but NVA forces were pressing in from the west and south of Quang Tri City and cutting Highway 1, which was the main north-south communication line. A fresh Marine Battalion was dispatched with the mission of keeping Highway 1 open, but they could maintain safe passage on the road only intermittently.

On 28 April several ARVN Regiments dissolved under the Communist artillery barrage and fled south of the Thach Han River. Commanders were able to re-establish some stability in their units, but it had become obvious that the outnumbered ARVN units must withdraw to the south. This withdrawal was begun in an orderly fashion on 1 May, but within a few hours Communist artillery introduced panic into the equation: even some of the best units began to crumble. Tanks and artillery pieces were abandoned as soldiers fled for their lives, and Highway 1 was soon choked with disarmed soldiers and civilians flooding south through a litter of discarded equipment under a continuous Communist artillery barrage.

The 1st Armor Brigade, the Ranger Battalions and the Marine Brigades had stayed together as units in the retreat, and they held back the Communist pursuit. But now all of Quang Tri Province was in Communist hands, and Hue was the next obvious target. To the west of Hue, the 324B NVA Division took FSB Bastogne on 28 April, a key installation for tactical control of the entire area. All South Vietnamese forces in the area then fell back to the east of FSB Birmingham. With four NVA divisions storming down from the north on the heels of the ARVN troops retreating from Quang Tri City, and a sixth NVA division known to be moving toward Hue from the A Shau Valley, things looked grim for the South Vietnamese forces.

On 3 May General Ngo Quang Truong was appointed the new Commander of I Corps. He was a shrewd, battle-toughened leader who proceeded immediately to Hue from IV Corps that day and took charge. He established his headquarters right at the front in Hue, rather than in the traditional, and safer, Corps Headquarters seat of Danang. On 4 May he shook up the entire command and control structure in I Corps, placing strong men he had brought with him in key positions. He brought the Marine Division and the 1st Infantry Division to the Hue vicinity, and within the next few weeks convinced Saigon to send him Airborne Brigades and Ranger Groups from the general reserve as well.

On 15 May the 1st Infantry Division helilifted troops to FSB Bastogne, where they caught the Communists off guard and retook the position. Within days, they also retook FSBs Birmingham and Checkmate: the tide began to turn. On the northern side, Communist armor-infantry attacks were occurring almost daily, but were constantly repelled by the ARVN Airborne and Marine Divisions. Meanwhile, the ARVN units that had arrived in Hue from Quang Tri had all their lost weapons, vehicles and equipment replaced from American stocks. American air strikes pounded the Communist troops as ARVN forces regrouped.

On 28 June two columns began to attack north in an attempt

to retake Quang Tri City and, eventually, all of the Province. One column was drawn from the Marine Division, the other from the Airborne Division, and they were strongly supported by their own artillery as well as by US tactical air cover. On 7 July the Airborne force reached the outskirts of Quang Tri City. It soon became obvious that the NVA would hold out to the last man, but there was really no choice: the South Vietnamese had to force the invading forces from their country.

At that time, the North Vietnamese had six divisions in the two northernmost provinces in South Vietnam: the 304, 308, 312, 320B, 324B and the 325. South Vietnam had only three divisions in the same highly contested area, although they were its best: the Marine, Airborne and 1st Infantry Divisions. Some very important South Vietnamese separate units were also there, including Ranger Groups, the 1st Armor Brigade, and numerous Artillery Battalions. But the trump card that helped South Vietnam retake Quang Tri was massive US air power.

Through July and August, B-52s and other American aircraft punished Communist positions all over I Corps, but especially in Quang Tri City. On 8 September a three-pronged attack was launched by the Airborne and Marine Divisions. On 14 September a Marine Battalion managed to penetrate one wall of the Citadel in the heart of Quang Tri City, the final Communist redoubt. The fight raged back and forth through the 15th, but that night the Marines got the upper hand. On the morning of the 16th, the South Vietnamese flag was raised over the Citadel, and by the 17th, all Communist troops had been driven out and 2767 casualties inflicted.

Farther south in I Corps, the 2nd ARVN Division was now counterattacking against the 2nd NVA Division and driving them back, while the refurbished 3rd ARVN Division was driving the 711th NVA Division from the Que Son Valley, a task accomplished by the middle of September. The military situation had stabilized in I Corps by the end of October, and South Vietnamese forces had regained most of the land the Communists had won at Easter.

Defending Kontum

The II Corps area of South Vietnam was at the same time the largest geographically—including nearly half the country's land area—and the least populated. The heavily jungled mountainous regions and high plateaus were inhabited primarily by a few hundred thousand members of the ethnic minority tribes named 'montagnards,' or 'mountain people,' by the French colonialists. Great rivalry and mistrust existed between them and the lowland ethnic Vietnamese, some three million of whom lived in II Corps, mostly in the narrow strip of fertile land along the coast. The interior held only a few large towns of any importance, notably Kontum and Pleiku in the north, Ban Me Thuot and Dalat in the south.

This sparse population pattern, combined with the limited number of roads, had long presented a most enticing prospect to the North Vietnamese: if Kontum and Pleiku could be taken, as well as Qui Nhon on the coast, then South Vietnam could be quickly and easily cut in half by securing Route 19 between the two areas, (one of only two east-west roads in all of II Corps). During the Easter Offensive, it was planned that the North Vietnamese NT-3 'Gold Star' Division, supported by local Viet Cong units, would concentrate on taking Qui Nhon, while the NVA 2nd and 320th Divisions and the 203rd Armor Regiment would come out of Laos and take Kontum and Pleiku.

The South Vietnamese forces in II Corps were the 22nd and 23rd Divisions and one mobile Ranger Group of 11 battalions. The Rangers were deployed in camps along the border, the 23rd Division at Ban Me Thuot and the 22nd was divided between Kontum in the Highlands and Qui Nhon on the coast. Ranger or Airborne Battalions from the General Reserve in Saigon were also occasionally sent to the area to handle increased Communist activity. In early February, intelligence showed a major Communist buildup in the Tan Canh-Dakto area north of Kontum. The 22nd Division Headquarters element, as well as two of its regiments and two armored cavalry squadrons, were moved there in February. In addition, a brigade of Airborne troops arrived from Saigon in the middle of March and occupied several FSBs to the north of Kontum on 'Rocket Ridge.'

A number of Communist attacks by elements of the 2nd and 320th NVA Divisions hit these FSBs in early April, but they were easily repelled. By this time, major invasions were taking place in I and III Corps, and several battalions of Airborne troops were taken out of II Corps to deal with those situations. Then, on 12 April, the 320th NVA Division launched a tank-supported human-wave attack, preceded by a heavy artillery barrage, against FSB Charlie. The defending Airborne battalion held out all day, but was thrown out during the night. FSB Delta was then assailed by heavy rocket and artillery fire, and a few days later fell to another tank-supported infantry rush. Communist casualties during these assaults were harrowing, but they seemed oblivious to the cost. Within a week, ARVN forces abandoned FSBs 5 and 6 without a fight, ceding the all-important high ground of Rocket Ridge to Communist forces. The two regiments of the 22nd ARVN Division in Tan Canh and Dakto were pummelled by North Vietnamese artillery. On 23 April the 2nd NVA Division streamed into Tan Canh, driving the ARVN troops before it. The next day, they attacked the 22nd ARVN Division Headquarters compound in Dakto, killing the Division Commander and much of his staff, and all organized defense quickly dissolved. Remnants of the 22nd Division fled toward Kontum out of control. Meanwhile, on the coast, the NVA 3rd Division had cut Highway 1, and controlled vast areas of the lowlands. Now the danger of South Vietnam's being cut in half was very real, and Kontum became a crucial location for both sides.

On 28 April the 23rd Division was moved from Ban Me Thuot to Kontum, where they joined the two regiments of the 22nd that had not been at Dakto. Four Ranger battalions were deployed on roads north of Kontum, and US air strikes pounded NVA forces north of them. The remainder of the Airborne Brigade that was still in II Corps was moved to I Corps in late April, further weakening Kontum's defenses. During the first week of May, the Ranger battalions north of Komtum were driven back by the 320th NVA Division. The

Rangers and the 23rd ARVN Division, together with some local Regional and Popular Forces, formed a perimeter defense around Kontum. On 14 May they were hit by a combined attack by the 2nd and 320th NVA Divisions.

Unlike the attacks on Rocket Ridge, Tan Canh and Dakto, the Communists did not begin their attack with artillery barrages. Instead, the 48th and 64th Regiments of the 320th moved down Route 14 from the northwest with tank columns on either side of the road. The 28th Regiment of the NVA B-3 Front attacked the 44th Regiment of the ARVN 23rd Division, while the 1st Regiment of the NVA 2nd Division attacked the 53rd Regiment of the ARVN 23rd Division. South of the city, the 141st Regiment of the NVA 2nd Division attacked Regional and Popular Forces entrenched along the Dak Bla River. But the two regiments of the 320th NVA Division ran into a wall. They had probably expected the ARVN troops to break and run, as they had in the Dakto region, but that didn't happen. Instead, they knocked out a number of Communist tanks with shoulder-fired rockets and pounded the attacking forces with air and artillery attacks. Communist forces hitting other parts of town were having no more success, and within a few hours the attacks were broken off.

Now the Communist artillery and rocket attacks commenced, and at nightfall the attack from the north was renewed with vigor. An NVA battalion slipped between the 44th and the 53rd Regiments, and the Communists began pouring troops through this breach. The 44th and 53rd tried to stretch to cover the gap between their lines, but it seemed beyond their ability. In desperation, the 23rd Division commander called for a diversion of a pre-planned B-52 strike, which normally would have required that friendly forces be pulled back an hour before delivery time. As this was impossible, one B-52 strike went in 20 minutes after the call went out, another less than half an hour later.

The earth was churned under the devastation of their bomb loads, and the whole city shook as the ARVN troops held their breaths. After the first strike, Communist reinforcements were poured into the gouged-out bomber tracks over the bodies of their comrades. After the second strike, there was only silence. At dawn ARVN reconnaissance forces moved through the area, where they found hundreds of Communist bodies littering the freshly ploughed fields.

Over the next few days, ARVN defenders reduced the size of their perimeter, tightening and strengthening their belt around the city. Their defenses were liberally sprinkled with LAW antitank weapons and TOW wire-guided missiles, and the defenders were increasingly confident they could hold. NVA probing attacks occurred continually around the city, but were uniformly repulsed. On several occasions, Communist troops were able to force their way between positions held by neighboring ARVN regiments, but the division reserve armored cavalry squadron was sent into the breach and managed to hold until air attacks could be brought to bear.

Meanwhile, on 21 May, a major effort was launched from Pleiku to clear Route 14 to Kontum. The 2nd and 6th Ranger Groups attacked north, supported by air strikes, but Communist blocking forces were well entrenched across the road, and their supporting artillery barrages stopped the rescue effort cold. The NVA was preparing its forces for one last throw of the dice, and knew that it must either take Kontum or withdraw from the artillery and air attacks. At first light on 25 May, Communist tanks and infantry units poured into the northeast sector of town, where they gained a firm foothold. A counterattack by one battalion of the 44th and eight ARVN tanks stopped the NVA advance, but could not dislodge it. At nightfall, the 64th NVA Regiment penetrated between the 53rd and 45th ARVN Regiments, and another diverted B-52 strike was needed to stop it.

On 27 May all defending units were frontally attacked by the NVA. The 23rd ARVN Division Commander brought his defenses in closer during the afternoon. By nightfall, ARVN troops were well established in prepared fallback positions, and B-52 strikes were brought in on their heels, smashing Communist troops as they moved up. Throughout 28 and 29 May, B-52 strikes hammered NVA positions; on 30 May a counterattack north by the 44th, 53rd and 45th ARVN Regiments made good headway. The B-52 strikes intensified during the night, and by noon of the next day, it was apparent that the 2nd and 320th NVA Divisions had had enough. Their withdrawal was complete. Route 14 between Pleiku and Kontum was reopened, and the Communist Easter Offensive was stopped in II Corps far earlier than it was in the other two areas of South Vietnam where major invasions took place.

The Siege of An Loc

The third area invaded by Communist forces was III Corps, which consisted of 11 provinces around Saigon, the national capital. South Vietnamese forces there included three Infantry Divisions, the 5th, 18th and 25th, and three Ranger Groups, the 3rd, 5th and 6th. By 1971 these forces had driven the North Vietnamese 5th, 7th and 9th Divisions out of III Corps and across the border into Cambodia. Intelligence in early 1972 showed that the 9th NVA Division planned to take Binh Long Province and establish An Loc as the capital city for the Communist 'Provisional Revolutionary Government' for all of South Vietnam. This was not fully believed at first, but as events were to show, it was precisely what the North Vietnamese intended.

On 2 April the 24th NVA Regiment (Separate) attacked FSB Lac Long near the Cambodian border in Tay Ninh Province with massed tanks and infantry. It soon fell. Saigon immediately ordered all outposts along the border abandoned, and withdrew its troops to stronger positions in the interior. On 4 April the NVA 5th Division attacked Loc Ninh, which fell to a column of some 30 tanks on 6 April. The ARVN 5th Division Commander ordered Task Force 52 to send one of its two battalions to the rescue, but before they could reach Loc Ninh, it had fallen, and superior NVA forces drove TF52 south to An Loc.

On 5 April two battalions of the 3rd Ranger Group had been helilifted into An Loc, clearly the next Communist target. The 1st Airborne Brigade attempted to open Route 13 from the south to An Loc, but they were stopped near the town by the 7th NVA Division in solid blocking positions.

On 7 April the An Loc airstrip at Quan Loi fell to Communist forces, which meant that An Loc was cut off from the outside except by helicopter or parachute. The siege of An Loc had begun. There were some 3000 ARVN troops there by this time, including Regional and Popular Forces, and some 6000 civilians who had not fled. All supplies to the military, as well as food for the civilians, now had to come by high-risk air transportation.

On 13 April Communist artillery barrages began to hit An Loc. Armored columns to the north drove ARVN defenders back, but at the edge of town, several NVA tanks were knocked out by shoulder-launched antitank weapons, and the attack stalled. Then the 271st and 272nd Regiments of the 9th NVA Division attacked from the west, but for two days they were held off by 5th ARVN Division troops and artillery and air strikes. On 14 April the 1st Airborne Brigade was helilifted into town, adding significantly to the strength of the defense component, and the 9th NVA Division withdrew their attacking forces.

On 19 April a renewed NVA attack on An Loc managed to take the northern half of town with the help of tanks and artillery, but they were stopped in the afternoon. A fierce point-blank artillery, armor and house-to-house infantry battle raged, and US bombing attacks smashed the numerically superior Communist forces. On 25 April Communist fire destroyed the hospital, further complicating matters for the defenders. Distribution of air-dropped food and other supplies was not always uniform, so that hunger and low supplies of ammunition began to play meaningful roles.

On 1 May the 5th NVA Division prepared to attack the southern side of An Loc, and was joined by the 7th NVA Division, which had left its blocking positions on Route 13 to the South. The 9th NVA Division still held the northern half of An Loc, and things looked bad for the defenders. Continuous air strikes, including B-52 missions, were being directed against Communist positions, causing them considerable delay in their preparations. On 11 May, however, after several hours of heavy artillery fire, the Communist attack was launched on all fronts. But massive air strikes were waiting, and the real turning point probably came around 9:00 AM, when the first B-52 strike hit Communist forces. Altogether, 30 B-52 strikes hit the NVA within the next 24 hours, with tactical fighter-bomber strikes between. The Communist positions were literally pulverized.

On 14 May another massed armor-infantry attack on all sides was launched by the three NVA Divisions, but again, the response was the same: B-52s crushed their attacks and sent them streaming from the field of battle. The defenders retook much of the northern part of town with little resistance, and by 17 May they controlled most of the original area. On 20 May the airstrip was retaken, and reinforcements poured into town. On 12 June troops arrived from Saigon on Route 13, and the An Loc region was again firmly under South Vietnamese Government control.

The autumn of 1972 was truly a triumphant time for the South Vietnamese military: they had been tested in the furnace of invasion by massive armor-supported conventional forces and found worthy. Truly, it seemed, they had earned their freedom from Communist domination and the right to a society where personal freedoms might grow and flourish. But it is most important not to ignore the key trump card that always won the day for South Vietnam: waves of American B-52 bombers.

THE FALL OF
SOUTH VIETNAM

By the fall of 1972, the three-pronged offensive launched at Easter by the North Vietnamese had been thrown back, and most of the south Vietnamese territory that had fallen to them had been retaken. The South Vietnamese were increasingly reluctant to sign the so-called 'Paris Agreements' with North Vietnam, the Viet Cong and the United States, which would supposedly end the war on grounds favorable to them. But more important to the Americans, these agreements, signed by the South Vietnamese, would lend at least the appearance of grace and good faith to the withdrawal of US troops from Indochina. The United States exerted considerable pressure on the South Vietnamese to sign, and finally threatened to sign without them and truly abandon them to their fate. Their leaders were given repeated assurances by then-President Nixon, both verbally and in writing, that the United States would continue to support them, and if the North Vietnamese committed serious violations of the cease-fire, American military forces would immediately be used to punish the transgressors.

Seeing little option, the South Vietnamese, on 27 January 1973; signed the agreements, which called, among other things, for an 'inplace' cease-fire. This left the South Vietnamese open to 'land-grab' tactics by the Communists, and the cease-fire quickly dissolved. By March of 1973, the

American pilots and other soldiers held as POWs by the North Vietnamese were released, and the US Congress seemed to want to wash its hands of Vietnamese involvement. In 1973 South Vietnam received $2.8 billion in US aid. In 1974 this fell to $1.1 billion and in 1975 to $300 million. Suddenly, every bullet counted.

After the Easter Offensive of 1972, the ARVN Airborne and Marine Divisions, both of which had long formed the primary South Vietnamese General Reserve forces, remained deployed in I Corps. Ammunition and other supplies were severely constrained for all South Vietnamese units, and they formed a thin line of defense stretched across contested areas of the country. The South Vietnamese had no reserves or even any scheduled defensive fall-back positions for their forces, and they remained convinced that if any North Vietnamese attacks were launched, American forces would quickly come flying to the rescue. This was not merely the result of President Nixon's assurances: they simply could not believe that the US would abandon the enormous investment it had made in South Vietnam.

But politics called a different tune than they expected. By August 1973 the US Congress had forced Nixon to cease all military action in or over Indochina. In November Congress passed the War Powers Resolution over President Nixon's veto, severely restricting the President's power to conduct war without Congressional approval. It was increasingly apparent that such approval would not be readily forthcoming in the event of another North Vietnamese invasion of South Vietnam. In addition, Nixon had become fatally ensnared in the coils of Watergate, and his concern over the fate of South Vietnam was rapidly dwindling.

Cease-fire violations by both sides became routine in 1973 and 1974. The North Vietnamese also spent this period expanding the network of roads that made up the Ho Chi Minh Trail, and were soon able to quickly and efficiently move supplies and reinforcements into South Vietnam. Their support system had been dramatically simplified when American bombing raids on their lines of communication ended in 1973, shortening a resupply trip of months into days.

Directly north of Saigon was Phuoc Long, the northernmost Province in III Corps. Sparsely populated and heavily jungled, Phuoc Long was wedged against the Cambodian border and was largely inaccessible to the ARVN. Because of geographical limitations, the South Vietnamese Government had long considered it virtually indefensible in the event of a strong attack against it by North Vietnamese forces.

In late 1974 two North Vietnamese Divisions with strong tank and artillery support moved into Phuoc Long and soon surrounded the Province capital city. By December resupply had to be made by air or by armored convoy. Two Ranger battalions were sent in as reinforcements at the end of December, but on 6 January 1975, South Vietnamese forces in Phuoc Long were overwhelmed, and the entire Province fell under North Vietnamese control.

In their defense of Phuoc Long, the South Vietnamese Air Force had lost 20 planes to anti-aircraft fire, including the highly accurate SA-7 missiles. This invasion had been a clear violation of the cease-fire, and the Province's collapse made it blatant. Even so, there was no reaction from American forces; it was becoming increasingly apparent that there would be none under similar circumstances in the future. The United States seemed to have abandoned their erstwhile allies, and the North Vietnamese were no doubt encouraged.

After Phuoc Long fell, however, the North Vietnamese paused and did not attempt to expand their control beyond the Province borders. This territorial victory was the most important precursor to the major North Vietnamese assault destined to conquer all of South Vietnam. The main bout would not begin until the attack against Ban Me Thuot, in the Central Highlands region of II Corps, on 10 March 1975.

All of II Corps was still defended by two divisions, the 22nd and the 23rd, as well as seven Ranger groups (each of regimental size), an armored brigade and local Regional and Popular Forces. Most of these troops were in the northern portion of II Corps, around Kontum, or along the narrow coastal strip of arable land, a traditional Communist stronghold. Only one regiment of the 23rd Division was in Ban Me Thuot in southern II Corps.

The North Vietnamese maintained five divisions, as well as 15 independent regiments of armored, artillery, anti-aircraft and engineer troops in II Corps. By the beginning of March, they had encircled Ban Me Thuot with three divisions, the 320th, the 316th and the F-10, and began to cut all road traffic into that town—and on most other roads throughout II Corps. Previous to this, South Vietnamese intelligence had shown that the North Vietnamese were not prepared to launch an all-out offensive similar to that of Easter 1972 until some time in 1976, but that meanwhile, they would pester and grab wherever they could. This encirclement of Ban Me Thuot occurred at the same time that very strong signals from prisoners, radio intercepts, captured documents and other sources showed a major offensive was to be launched in II Corps by the North Vietnamese.

Before dawn on 10 May, the 316th and 320th NVA Divisions attacked Ban Me Thuot, over-running most of the defenses in town by midday. The 53rd Regiment of the 23rd ARVN Division was isolated and under heavy attack at the airport. Over the next few days, the other two regiments of the 23rd were flown into a town some 20km away, but a strange breakdown in discipline began to occur: Ban Me Thuot was the 'rear area' for the 23rd, where Division Headquarters and most dependents of the 23rd's soldiers were located. As they landed near Ban Me Thuot, men of the 23rd began to desert in droves, panic-stricken, to try to rescue their families. This powerful protective drive on the part of its soldiers would contribute heavily to the dissolution of the South Vietnamese State over the next few months.

Before the attack had begun, President Thieu had ordered the Airborne Division—his primary traditional Reserve force—returned to Saigon from I Corps, where it had been deployed for nearly two years. This redeployment began on 10 March, the day the attack on Ban Me Thuot was launched, and the withdrawal of these elite forces from I Corps at the same time as a massive Communist attack in the Central Highlands fanned rumors of a secret 'deal' whereby the northern portion of South Vietnam would be ceded to the Communists without a fight.

This turned out to be more than just the idle rumors that had long plagued the South Vietnamese Government: after this massive Communist attack in the mountains of II Corps, President Thieu made a dramatic change in strategy. He decided to concede the sparsely inhabited sections of I and II Corps to the North Vietnamese and withdraw his forces to the more heavily populated regions along the coast.

On 13 March President Thieu ordered the Commander of I Corps to formulate immediate plans to withdraw his forces from most of I Corps and use them to form a tight cordon around Danang, the only region of the Corps to be defended. On 14 March Thieu met with the II Corps Commander and directed that the remainder of the 'Regular' forces (part of the 23rd Division, the Ranger Groups and the Armored Brigade) be moved from the Pleiku-Kontum areas to the coast within a few days; the Regional and Popular Forces would be left behind to face the invading North Vietnamese Divisions. No dependents of the soldiers involved were to accompany them on the move, which was to be made on the long-abandoned Route 7B that led through the mountains from Pleiku to Tuy Hoa on the coast. This road selection turned out to be a poor tactical decision, for Route 7B was in a bad state of repair. Heavily mined by both sides, with many of its bridges dangerous or unusable, the chosen path would only add to the magnitude of the tragic slaughter ahead.

On 16 March the withdrawal from Pleiku and Kontum on Route 7B began. The troops were to make their move from the 16th through the 18th, with most of the Rangers leaving last and providing rear security. But the road-opening operation went more slowly than anticipated, and on the first day the column was blocked by a destroyed bridge in Cheo Reo. By midday on the 16th, the column of soldiers on the road had mingled with a flood of civilian refugees who refused to be left behind to be ruled by the Communists.

On the 17th the North Vietnamese managed to move much of their 320th Division up to Route 7B, where they rained death on South Vietnamese civilian and military alike. ARVN Ranger Battalions were unable to bypass the choked refugees until the 20th, when they finally forced the road at great cost.

Although the entire movement had been planned for a three-day time frame, ARVN soldiers were still streaming down Route 7B on 1 April, when Tuy Hoa fell to the Communists. Only some 20,000 of the 60,000 troops scheduled to reach the coast ever got there; those who did were almost useless for combat. Only about 700 of the 7000 Rangers made it out alive, but it was due to their suicidal attacks on strong Communist positions that any South Vietnamese at all got to Tuy Hoa. Of the 400,000 civilian refugees fleeing in the face of the Communists, only about 100,000 got to the coast; the fate of the rest is unknown.

With the loss of Ban Me Thuot and the subsequent decision to abandon Pleiku and Kontum, all ARVN resistance in II Corps began to crumble. The 22nd Division in Binh Dinh Province was heavily attacked from the highlands to their west, then suddenly hit by waves of refugees from Quang Ngai to the north, followed by North Vietnamese tanks and artillery. They were driven south until 1 April, when the 2000 men left in the division (out of 10,000 a week earlier) were evacuated by sea from Qui Nhon. Meanwhile, the Communist F-10 Division was driving down Route 21 from Ban Me Thuot toward Nha Trang. On 17 March one brigade of the Airborne Division being evacuated from I Corps was inserted into a mountain pass on Route 21, where they stopped the Communist advance. After a week of heavy fighting and severe casualties, however, they were outflanked and forced to withdraw toward Nha Trang. On the 1st of April, the entire heavily populated coastal strip of II Corps was in a state of chaos. Although ARVN units had not yet been challenged for much of the land area involved, they were rapidly disintegrating as the Communist onslaught approached. Senior officers were fleeing to Saigon by air as fast as possible.

Meanwhile, I Corps had endured its own problems since early March. There were initially five ARVN Divisions there, including the elite Airborne Division (soon to be withdrawn), the Marine Division, an Armored Brigade and four Ranger Groups. The North Vietnamese maintained seven divisions in I Corps, as well as several others just across the DMZ in North Vietnam itself.

On 8 March the 324th NVA Division launched a heavy attack against Phu Bai, just south of Hue, but were stopped when they suffered heavy losses at the hands of the ARVN 2nd Division. At the same time, five NVA Battalions attacked Hue from the north, but they were repulsed by South Vietnamese Marines. As mentioned earlier, however, the ARVN Airborne Division was extracted beginning on 10 March, and as they pulled out, much of the civilian populace panicked. The roads were soon jammed with refugees racing south toward Hue and Danang. The departure of the Airborne fueled rumors of another political 'deal,' which turned out to be accurate: northern I Corps was to be abandoned to the Communists. The massacre of civilians by the North Vietnamese while they held Hue during the Tet Offensive of 1968 was vivid in the people's memory, and few of them would accept such a risk. As the refugees flooded south, massed NVA armor and infantry were on their heels.

By 20 March ARVN forces had been driven back to Hue. Next day the 325th NVA Division overran the ARVN 15th Ranger Group north of the Hai Van pass, thus cutting Highway 1, the main road between Hue and Danang. Discipline began to dissolve in Hue, and on 25 March, the order was given to evacuate the city by sea and abandon it to the Communists. But fewer than half the troops scheduled for evacuation arrived at the docks, and most were of little value upon their arrival in Danang. On 24 March an NVA armored column cut Route 1 between Danang and the city of Chu Lai to the south, and on 25 March Chu Lai fell to the Communists.

For South Vietnamese soldiers, it was their home that was falling to the invaders from the north, and family ties exerted ever-stronger claims. While some units were still in control, most were dissolving as the individual soldiers tried to save their families. Danang's defenders were now reduced to the ARVN 3rd Division, two Marine Brigades and various regional and popular forces, but the population of the city had been swollen to over a million by refugees, many of them armed deserters from ARVN units.

On 28 March Saigon told the I Corps Commander that NVA forces would attack Danang on 29 March, and ordered him to evacuate whatever troops he could by ship to Saigon. On 29 March, as Danang fell to North Vietnamese control, only about 6000 Marines (less than half the division) and some 4000 other assorted ARVN troops got aboard ships and eventually reached Saigon.

By 1 April I Corps and most of II Corps—more than half South Vietnam's territory—had been lopped off by the North Vietnamese Communists. III and IV Corps were to be defended by two Airborne Brigades and some 18,000 other disorganized ARVN troops evacuated by sea from I and II Corps. Indigenous units for the defense included six Infantry Divisions, two Armored Brigades, various Ranger Groups and Regional and Popular Forces. In IV Corps, the 7th, 9th, and 21st Divisions were all tied down by local Communist forces, a situation long nurtured by North Vietnam. During the first week in April, Communist forces in IV Corps drove north to Long An Province just south of Saigon, where they threatened to cut Highway 4, the Capital's main link with the rest of the Delta. Elements of the re-equipped 22nd Division that had been evacuated from II Corps were sent to Long An Province to try to prevent this, but they were eventually surrounded by Communist forces.

In III Corps the ARVN 25th Division was in the Tay Ninh area northwest of Saigon, where it was heavily engaged with Communist forces. The ARVN 5th Division was north of Saigon in Binh Duong Province, while the ARVN 18th Division was northeast of Saigon near Xuan Loc, where the last battle of the war for South Vietnam was to be fought.

For the defense of Saigon itself, a polyglot organization of Airborne, Rangers, Marines, and Regional and Popular Forces constituted perhaps two Divisions, but were probably too disorganized and demoralized to put up more than a token resistance. The South Vietnamese Air Force had been cut by more than half, and flew out of only four airfields left under their control: Can Tho in the Delta, Phan Rang on the coast in southern II Corps, and Tan Son Nhut and Bien Hoa in the Saigon area. The South Vietnamese Government still clung desperately to the fading hope that American troops would come to their rescue at the last minute, but their pleas for help were falling on deaf ears.

Pressure slackened during the first week in April, and the South Vietnamese Government decided to insert ARVN troops into the airport at Phan Rang and try to mount a counter-offensive. Two regiments from the ARVN 2nd Division that had been evacuated from I Corps and one Brigade of Airborne troops were landed there on 6 April. For three days they met little opposition, and on 10 April the Airborne Brigade was extracted and sent to Xuan Loc, where a major battle was developing. They were replaced by a Ranger Group, but on 15 April ARVN forces at Phan Rang were hit by waves of North Vietnamese infantry supported by tanks, which quickly overran them and extinguished the last ARVN presence in II Corps.

Meanwhile, on 8 April the ARVN 18th Division in Xuan Loc had become heavily engaged with two NVA Divisions. A regiment of the ARVN 5th Division, as well as the Airborne Brigade extracted from the expeditionary force at Phan Rang, were sent in as reinforcements while, over the ensuing week, two more NVA Divisions arrived to aid in the attack. The North Vietnamese used heavy artillery support and human-wave infantry attacks studded with tanks, but the ARVN forces were well dug in. They used the last of their air support—heavy C-130 transport aircraft that rolled 15,000-lb 'Daisy Cutter' bombs from their cargo bays onto the massed Communist ranks—with telling effect. However, the North Vietnamese forces had the South Vietnamese outgunned and outmanned. As their tactical air-support aircraft and weapons became depleted, the ARVN forces were unable to hold.

Outflanked and pounded by heavy artillery, the ARVN 18th Division and attached units withdrew on 21 April after having stopped the Communist flood for nearly two weeks. This was to be the last battle in defense of the Republic of Vietnam, and when it was lost, President Thieu resigned, signaling the end for even the last of the die-hard anti-Communists. Remaining ARVN units quickly dissolved, as politicians formed governments hourly. The mad scramble to get out of Saigon before the Communist arrival was on.

In retrospect, a key factor in the collapse of South Vietnam was that this was the home country of the ARVN soldiers fighting to defend it against Communism, and many of them felt a personal bond to the land of their ancestors that few Westerners can easily understand. When this was combined with the fact that the immediate families of South Vietnamese soldiers were often near their men, and so directly endangered by Communist invasions, it is perhaps more apparent why concerns other than military duty were important to South Vietnamese soldiers.

But the key to understanding the rapid collapse of the Republic of Vietnam lies with President Thieu's decision in early March to conduct a mass retreat, with no warning or preparations, of his Regular forces from the Kontum-Pleiku area. An organized retreat under enemy fire is the most difficult military maneuver there is; add to that ten times as many panicked civilians as military (many of them the soldiers' relatives) and the problems quickly become insurmountable. President Thieu would have been well advised to remember the rout of his best troops in a similar but simpler retreat, minus civilians, after Operation Lam Son 719 into Laos in 1971. His failure to learn that lesson ultimately cost him his state, as well as untold South Vietnamese military and civilian lives.

INDOCHINA SMOLDERS ON

The Never-ending War

Even after the 1 May 1975 triumphant parade of victorious North Vietnamese troops through the streets of Saigon—now Ho Chi Minh City—coils of war still writhed across the Indochinese Peninsula. On 12 May Americans were startled by a parting bite from Indochinese Communists.

That morning the old American tramp steamer *Mayaguez* was lumbering along the Cambodian coast from Hong Kong to Thailand when it was stopped and boarded by the crew of a Communist Cambodian gunboat. They then escorted it to Koh Tang Island some 35 miles from the mainland, but cries for help had gone out over the radio before the boarding, and a determined US Government intended to use this incident to show the world that America was not a paper tiger.

The *Mayaguez* crew was taken to the port of Kompong Som by fishing boat on 14 May, but the rescue forces being hurriedly assembled believed they were either still on their ship or on Koh Tang Island. A battalion of Marines was rushed to U Tapao US Air Force Base in Thailand on 14 May, and Air Force fighter bombers sank three Cambodian gunboats that day in a vain effort to interdict traffic between Koh Tang and mainland Cambodia.

In the early hours of 14 May, 228 Marines were flown the 200 miles between U Tapao and Koh Tang in 11 Air Force helicopters. The first landings were made at Koh Tang at 6:15

AM, and met unexpectedly heavy resistance. An hour later, three helicopter loads of Marines landed on the deck of an American destroyer, the USS *Wilson*, which then pulled up alongside the *Mayaguez*.

The Marines boarded her in true eighteenth-century style, but they found she was empty. Meanwhile, the force that landed at Koh Tang had walked into a buzz saw.

One unit was supposed to land on the western beach, while the rest of the assault force would land at a larger opening on the eastern side of the island. The first two helicopters destined for the eastern LZ were shot down, however, with one going into the surf, resulting in 13 deaths. Thirteen survivors from the craft swam out to sea, where they were eventually picked up by a US destroyer. The other helicopter had its tail rotor shot off on the beach, and the 20 Marines and four air-crew members from that craft spent the rest of the day huddled in a tight perimeter.

On the western side of the island, the first two helicopters were also shot up as they approached. One limped back to Thailand, but the other managed to disgorge its passengers before it crashed in the ocean, killing one of its four crew members. No more helicopters could get into the eastern LZ, so the four remaining were diverted to the west, where they landed safely.

Meanwhile, the crew of the *Mayaguez* had already been released and was heading back to their ship on a fishing boat, but the Americans didn't know that. At 9:00 AM planes off the American aircraft carrier USS *Coral Sea* bombed Ream Airfield in Cambodia, the Ream Naval Base and an oil refinery near Kompong Som. An hour later the fishing boat bearing the crew of the *Mayaguez* arrived at the *Wilson* and word went out that they were safe. Another 200 Marines went into Koh Tang to help remove those already there, but with the help of massive bombing, the extraction was complete by full dark. Total US casualties were 41 killed (including 23 in Thailand, when a helicopter crashed while preparing for the assault on Koh Tang) and 50 wounded, but the release of the crew was a welcome salve to sorely bruised American egos.

The *Mayaguez* incident, however, was only a sideshow to the main action in Indochina, which saw the Communist North Vietnamese swell with self-assurance during the late 1970s. Vietnamese leaders had long spoken of their right to rule all of Indochina, and before the decade was out, Ho Chi Minh's successors in Hanoi were to realize that dream. Laos fell under North Vietnamese control when the Lao People's Democratic Party, a puppet run from Hanoi, took over the country in December 1975. Although the Pathet Lao had long been the agents for the exercise of North Vietnamese will in Laos, in the early 1970s North Vietnamese troops had invaded the country and openly fought against the forces of the Royal Laotian Government. But the sparsely populated, heavily jungled mountains of Laos were far less of a prize than the fertile fields of Cambodia.

While the North Vietnamese were conquering South Vietnam, their Communist allies in Cambodia, the Khmer Rouge, were overthrowing the pro-Western government of Lon Nol. Once in power, North Vietnamese were unusually discreet in dealing with the vanquished: although they sent hundreds of thousands of former South Vietnamese enemies to 're-education camps,' there were few indications of the feared bloodbaths. In Cambodia, on the other hand, the new Communist ruler, Pol Pot, emptied the cities and attempted to uproot every vestige of civilization—no money, no books, no mail, no education, no cars, no electricity. While he was harshly returning the re-named state of Kampuchea to a subsistence agriculture existence, he ruthlessly slaughtered up to a quarter of the nation's eight million inhabitants. His action shocked the world, and 'bloodbath' was little more than a euphemism for what he did to his own people.

Over time, old ethnic rivalries between Vietnamese and Kampucheans began to reappear. In 1977 Khmer Rouge forces often raided Vietnamese border towns and kidnapped residents. Hanoi decided to punish them with a major raid deep into Kampuchea, but it was poorly carried off: tanks got lost or ran out of gas, and their crews had to be rescued by Vietnamese pilots flying helicopters left behind by the Americans. When they pulled back into Vietnam, the Khmer

Rouge were nipping at their heels and announcing to the world that they had driven the mighty Vietnamese Army out of their country. The Vietnamese regrouped and methodically planned an invasion that would not fail. But this time, rather than settle for punishing the Kampucheans, they would try to take the whole country and install a puppet government.

By December 1978 the Vietnamese Communists were ready. More than 100,000 experienced troops were poised on the border in twelve divisions, ready to slice through the 73,000 members of the Khmer Rouge. On 14 December two Vietnamese Divisions moved north across the border from Tay Ninh, slowly making their way north up Route 13 towards the town of Kratie. If this advance were allowed to continue, it would lop off the northeast quadrant of Kampuchea, a territory that had been controlled by North Vietnamese Communists for most of the preceding 10 or 15 years. This was the bait, and the Khmer Rouge swallowed it immediately, moving nearly half of their forces to defend the northeast section of the country.

On 25 December the main offensive was launched. Massive air and artillery strikes hammered the Khmer Rouge forces moving into the northeast sector, pinning them down or killing them outright. And while the defending forces were so occupied, Vietnamese forces poured across the border to the south. Two Vietnamese divisions swarmed north from Can Tho, quickly taking the town of Takeo and controlling Highways 3 and 4. Another division moved up Highway 1 through the Parrot's Beak virtually unopposed. Two more divisions out of Tay Ninh headed west for Kompong Chom, crossed the Mekong River with their armored vehicles on Soviet pontoon bridges and trapped a Khmer Rouge Division that was so stunned it surrendered without a fight.

Pnom Penh soon fell virtually without a fight, and Vietnamese forces sped up Highways 5 and 6 to the northwest, bypassing more Khmer Rouge soldiers. Meanwhile, back in the northeast sector, three divisions came racing west on Highway 19 from Pleiku and quickly took the town of Stung Treng. Two more divisions came south out of Laos, and suddenly the Khmer Rouge troops who had been tricked into the area and bypassed by Vietnamese invasions were facing more than they could handle. With little fight, they dissolved and either surrendered or made their way into the hills in small bands to wage guerrilla warfare against their new conquerors.

It had been a lightning stroke that would have made Rommel or Patton smile. After less than a month, the Vietnamese turned the bulk of their forces away from the last Khmer Rouge holdouts along the Thai border and went back into the countryside to mop up the units they had bypassed. Virtually every town and road in the country was under their control. The invasion force had included 18,000 Khmer Rouge dissidents, and one of them, Heng Samrin, was made the leader of the Vietnam-controlled puppet government of Kampuchea.

Pol Pot's defeated troops and their families have washed back and forth across the Thai border ever since then. While they occasionally boast of plans to defeat the Vietnamese, that would be a most unlikely outcome. The Vietnamese conquest of Kampuchea, however, highlighted a serious breach in their relations with the People's Republic of China. While Vietnam has edged ever closer to the Sovet Union since 1976, Pol Pot and the Khmer Rouge were the special protegés of the Chinese, who in any case disliked the idea of Vietnam controlling Laos and Kampuchea.

The ethnic Chinese living in Vietnam began to bear the brunt of Vietnamese displeasure with the rulers of the People's Republic of China. In the summer of 1978, several hundred thousand of them fled South Vietnam, along with hundreds of thousands of other refugees, in small open boats. Some of these refugees reached China, some Indonesia, Malaysia, or the Philippines. But many were attacked, robbed and murdered by pirates. Others simply drifted without food until they starved to death. It has been estimated that about half of the so-called 'Boat People' die before they reach dry ground, and even those who are rescued often end up in little more than prison camps in countries that do not welcome them.

In late 1978 Chinese aid to Vietnam was cut off, and Vietnam grew closer still to the Soviet Union. January 1979 saw brief battles along the Chinese-Vietnamese border, and on 17 February, several hundred thousand Chinese troops washed into Vietnam on three fronts: in the west, Chinese forces threatened the town of Lai Chau on the Black River; in the north, they moved toward Ha Giang; and in the northeast, they took the town of Lang Son and soon had major forces poised on the edge of open plains that led directly to Hanoi.

The Vietnamese fought hard, however, and within a few weeks, the Chinese had lost over 50,000 killed—nearly as many deaths as American soldiers had suffered in more than six years of US troop involvement in Vietnam. But the Chinese did not wish to go any deeper into Vietnam, and announcing that they had 'taught Vietnam a lesson,' they withdrew their troops.

Since then Vietnam has increased its army of occupation in Kampuchea to over 200,000, and this has enabled them to solve several problems at once. The young men of South Vietnam who might be expected to foment revolution at home against their new Communist masters are drafted and sent to Kampuchea. Once there, they serve under rigid discipline at the direction of North Vietnamese sergeants, and are often killed or maimed while fighting Vietnam's inglorious war against the people of Kampuchea.

While Vietnamese forces occasionally stray into Thailand in pursuit of Khmer Rouge rebels, most knowledgeable observers doubt that Vietnam would ever seriously invade Thailand, for both the Chinese and the Americans have promised to support Thailand in that eventuality. However, attempting to predict the actions of Vietnamese Communists has led to the downfall of many Westerners in the past. All that can be safely said is that the Vietnam War now smolders on throughout all of Indochina, and it shows no signs of dying soon.

INDEX